CALL HIM BY NO NAME

For he had no name. He had no language. For all he knew he was the only living being in the billions of light-years of space across the galaxy. And he was the only traveler in space.

Call him a thinking rock, a sentient planetoid.

Call him a rogue.

Call him a rogue in space . . .

Bantam Science Fiction and Fantasy
Ask your bookseller for the books you have missed

ROGUE IN SPACE
Fredric Brown

ROGUE IN SPACE
A Bantam Book

PRINTING HISTORY

Dutton edition published February 1957

Bantam edition | December 1957
2nd printing .... August 1971
3rd printing .... December 1978

*Bantam Books are published by Bantam Books, Inc. Its trade-
mark, consisting of the words "Bantam Books" and the por-
trayal of a bantam, is registered in the United States Patent
Office and in other countries. Marca Registrada. Bantam
Books, Inc., 666 Fifth Avenue, New York, New York 10019.*

ROGUE IN SPACE

CALL him by no name, for he had no name. He did not know the meaning of *name*, or of any other word. He had no language, for he had never come into contact with any other living being in the billions of light-years of space that he had traversed from the far rim of the galaxy, in the billions of years that it had taken him to make that journey. For all he knew or had ever known he was the only living being in the universe.

He had not been born, for there was no other like him. He was a piece of rock a little over a mile in diameter, floating free in space. There are myriads of such small worlds but they are dead rock, inanimate matter. He was *aware*, and an entity. An accidental combination of atoms into molecules had made him a living being. To our present knowledge such an accident has happened only twice in infinity and eternity; the other such event took place in the primeval ooze of Earth, where carbon atoms formed sentient life that multiplied and evolved.

Spores from Earth had drifted across space and had seeded the two planets nearest to it, Mars and Venus, and when a million years later man had landed on those planets he found vegetable life waiting for him there, but that vegetable life, although it had evolved quite differently from vegetable life as man knew it, had still originated on Earth. Nowhere but on earth had life originated to evolve and multiply.

The entity from the far side of the galaxy did not multiply. He remained unique and alone. Nor did he evolve except in the sense that his awareness and his knowledge grew. Without sensory organs, he learned to perceive the universe about him. Without language, he learned to understand its principles and its mechanics and how to make use of them to move through space freely, and to do many other things.

Call him a thinking rock, a sentient planetoid.

Call him a rogue, in the biological sense of the word rogue: an accidental variation.

Call him a rogue in space.

He roamed space but he did not search for other life, other consciousness, for he had long since assumed that none existed.

He was not lonely, for he had no concept of loneliness. He had no concept of good and evil, for a lone being can know neither; morality arises only in our attitude toward others. He had no concept of emotion, unless a desire to increase awareness and knowledge (we call it curiosity) can be called an emotion.

Now, after billions of years—but neither young nor old—he found himself nearing a small yellow sun that had nine planets circling about it.

There are many such.

CHAPTER TWO

CALL him Crag; it was the name he was using and it will serve as well as any name. He was a smuggler and a thief and a killer. He'd been a spaceman once and had a metal hand to show for it. That, and a taste for exotic liquors and a strong aversion for work. Work would have been futile for him in any case; he would have had to work a week, at anything but crime, to buy a single binge on even the cheapest of the nepenthes that alone made life worth living. He knew good from evil but cared not a grain of Martian sand for either of them. He was not lonely for he had made himself self-sufficient by hating everyone.

Especially now, because they had him. And of all places here in Albuquerque, the center of the Federation and the toughest spot on five planets to beat a rap. Albuquerque, where justice was more crooked than crime, where a criminal didn't have a chance unless he belonged to the machine. Independent operators were not wanted and did not last long. He should never have come here, but he'd been tipped to a sure thing and had taken a chance. He knew now that the tipster had been part of the machine and that the tip had been a trap to entice him here. He hadn't even had time to case the job he'd come here to do—if such a job had existed at all except in the tipster's imagination. He'd been picked up leaving the airport and searched. Almost an ounce of *nepthin* had been found in his pocket, and it had really been there, concealed in the false bottom of a pack of cigarettes. The cigarettes had been given him by the talkative cigarette salesman who had sat next to him on the plane, as a free sample of a new brand his company was introducing. *Nephthin* was bad stuff; possession of it, however acquired, was a psychable offense. It had been a perfect frame. They had him cold.

3

There was only one question left, and that was whether they'd give him twenty in the penal colony on bleak Callisto or whether they'd send him to the psycher.

He sat on the cot in his cell and wondered which would happen. It made a big difference. Life in the penal colony might turn out to be better than no life at all and there would always be the chance, however slender, of escape. But the thought of the psycher was intolerable. Before he'd let them send him to the psycher, he decided, he'd kill himself or get himself killed trying to escape.

Death was something you could look in the face and laugh at. But not the psycher. Not the way Crag looked at it. The electric chair of a few centuries before merely killed you; the psycher did something much worse than that. It *adjusted* you, unless it drove you crazy. Statistically, one time out of nine it drove you stark mad, and for this reason it was used only in extreme cases, for crimes that would have been punishable by death back in the days of capital punishment. And even for such crimes, including *nephthin* possession, it was not mandatory; the judge chose between it and the alternative maximum sentence of twenty years on Callisto. Crag shuddered at the thought that if the psycher ever *were* perfected, if that one chance out of nine of being lucky were eliminated, it would probably be made mandatory for much lesser crimes.

When the psycher worked, it made you normal. It made you normal by removing from your mind all the memories and experiences which had led you into aberration from the norm. *All* your memories and experiences, the good ones as well as the bad.

After the psycher, you started from scratch as far as personality was concerned. You remembered your skills; you knew how to talk and feed yourself, and if you'd known how to use a slide rule or play a flute you still knew how to use a slide rule or play a flute.

But you didn't remember your name unless they told you. And you didn't remember the time you were tortured for three days and two nights on Venus before the rest of the crew found you and took you away from the animated vegetables who didn't like meat in any form and particularly in human form. You didn't remember the time you were spacemad or the time you had to go nine days without water. You didn't remember anything that had ever happened to you.

You started from scratch, a different person.

And while Crag could face dying, he could not and would not face the thought of his body walking around afterwards, animated by a well-adjusted stranger whose very guts he would hate. If necessary he'd kill that well-adjusted stranger by killing, before the stranger could take it over, the body which the stranger would make do and think things that Crag would never do or think.

He knew that he could do it, but it would not be easy; the weapon he carried was better adapted to killing others than to suicide. It takes a lot of courage to kill oneself with a bludgeon.

Even so efficient a bludgeon as Crag's metal left hand. Looking at that hand, no one had ever guessed that it weighed twelve pounds instead of a few ounces. Since the metal was flesh colored, one had to look closely to see that it was an artificial hand at all. If one did notice, since all artificial members had for over a century been made of duralloy, one assumed that Crag's hand was similarly made. Duralloy is a fraction of the weight of magnesium, not much heavier than balsa wood. And Crag's hand *was* duralloy on the outside, but it was reinforced with steel and heavily weighted with lead. Not a hand you'd want to be slapped in the face with, even lightly. But long practice and considerable strength enabled Crag to carry and use it as though it weighed the three or four ounces you'd expect it to weigh.

Nor had anyone ever guessed that it was detachable, since all similar artificial hands—or feet or arms or legs—were surgically and permanently attached to their wearers. That was why they had not taken it away from him when he was arrested nor when he had been stripped and given prison garb here at the jail. A renegade surgeon hiding out in Rio had fixed that part of it for him (Crag had fabricated the hand himself) by grafting and manipulating muscle tissue at the stump of the wrist so that holding it on was automatic and involuntary. But by willing the muscles to relax, the heavy hand was instantly detachable, and became a missile that his right hand could throw, after long practice, with deadly accuracy. One might well say that Crag had a long reach, for one blow. And one blow was always sufficient, against a single antagonist.

It was the only weapon Crag ever carried.

A voice from a grill in the ceiling of the cell said, "Your trial has been called for fourteen hours. That is ten minutes from now. Be ready."

Crag glanced upward and made a rude noise at the grill. Since it was strictly a one-way communicator, the grill paid no attention.

Crag walked over to the window and stood looking down at the vast sprawling city of Albuquerque, third largest city in the solar system, second largest city on Earth. Running diagonally off to the southeast he could see the bright ribbon of the shuttlejet track that led to Earth's largest spaceport, forty miles away.

The window was not barred but the transparent plastic of the pane was tough stuff. He could probably batter it out with his left hand but would need wings to continue an escape in that direction. His cell was on the top floor of Fedjude, the Federation Judical Building, thirty stories high, the wall sheer and the windows flush. He could only commit suicide that way, and suicide could wait, as long as there was even a chance of getting the penal colony instead of the psycher.

He hated it, that corrupt city, worse in its way than Mars City, vice city of the solar system. Albuquerque was not a fleshpot, but it was the center of intrigue between the Guilds and the Gilded. Politics rampant upon a field of muck, and everybody, except the leaders, caught in the middle, no matter which side they supported or even if they tried to remain neutral.

The voice from the ceiling said, "Your door is now unlocked. You will proceed to the end of the corridor outside it, where you will meet the guards who will escort you to the proper room."

Through the windowpane Crag caught the faint silver flash of a spaceship coming in, heard dimly the distant thunder of its jets. He waited a few seconds until it was out of sight.

But no longer, for he knew that, in a small way, this order was a test. He could wait here and force the guards to come and get him, but if he did so, and particularly if he tried to resist when they did come, his recalcitrance would be reported, would be taken into consideration when sentence was pronounced. It could make the difference between Callisto and the psycher.

So he opened the now unlocked door and went out into the corridor and along it; there was only one way to go. A hundred yards along it two green-uniformed guards waited for him. They were armed with holstered heat-guns; they stood before the first door that otherwise would have stopped his progress.

He didn't speak to them nor they to him. They stepped apart and he fell in between them. The door opened automatically as they approached it, but he knew that it would not have opened for him alone.

He knew too that he could have killed both quite easily, literally and figuratively offhand. A backhand blow to the face or forehead of the guard to his left and then a quick swing across to the other one; both would have died without a chance to draw their weapons, without knowing what had happened to them. But getting past all the other barriers and safeguards would be something else again. Too remote a chance to consider now, before he had heard the sentence. So he walked quietly between them down the ramp to the floor below and along other corridors to the room where he was to be tried. And through the door.

He was the last arrival, if you didn't count the two guards who came in behind him.

The room was moderately large, but there were only an even dozen people in it, counting Crag and his two guards. Trial procedure had been greatly simplified under the Federation, although, in theory at least, it was as fair and impartial as it had ever been.

A judge, wearing an ordinary business suit, sat behind an ordinary businessman's desk, his back against one wall. The two lawyers, one for the prosecution and one for the defense, had smaller desks, one on each side of the judge's. The five jurors sat in comfortable chairs along one wall. Against a third wall, the sound technician had his machines and his rack of tapes. The defendant's chair was placed diagonally so it faced halfway between the judge and the jury. There were no spectators present and no reporters, although the trial was not secret; the entire trial would be recorded on tape and after the trial copies of the tape would be immediately available to representatives of any authorized news disseminating medium applying in advance for them.

None of this was new to Crag for he had been tried once before—acquitted that time because four of the five jurors, the number necessary for either conviction or acquittal, had decided that the evidence was insufficient. But one thing did surprise him and that was the identity of the judge. The judge was Olliver.

The surprising thing about that was not the fact that Olliver had been the judge who had presided at Crag's previous trial six years ago—that could be coincidence or it could be because Olliver had applied, a judge's privilege, to sit at this trial because of his previous interest in Crag. The surprising thing was that Olliver would be sitting as judge, at present, in *any* ordinary criminal case. In the six years since Crag's first trial, Olliver had become a very important man.

Judge Olliver, although less rabidly conservative than most members of the Syndicate Party—popularly known as the Gilded—had risen high in that party and had been its candidate for Coordinator of North America, second most important political office in the solar system, at the election only six months ago. True, he had lost the election, but he had polled more votes than any Syndicate candidate had in North America for almost a century. Surely he would have gained an important enough position in the party to have lifted himself above the routine work of judging criminal cases.

In Crag's opinion, he certainly should have, for although Crag hated him as a man, he had reluctant admiration for Olliver. Politically cynical though Crag was, he thought Olliver came nearer to being a statesman than any other man in politics. It seemed to Crag that the Syndicate Party would now be grooming Olliver for a try at the really top job—System Coordinator—at the next election. In North America, as on Mars, the Guild Party had a strong majority, but throughout the system as a whole the two parties were fairly equally balanced and the System Coordinator's job and the majority of seats on the System Council were tossups in any election. Surely Olliver, by his showing in an election where the odds had been strongly against him, had earned himself a chance at running for the higher job, which he would be almost certain to win.

As to why Crag hated Olliver personally, the answer lay in the blistering tongue-lashing Olliver had administered to him after the previous trial in the private conversation between the judge and the accused that was customary at the end of a trial whether or not the accused was found guilty. Olliver had called him names that Crag had not forgotten.

Now Crag faced him again, knowing that this time the jury would certainly find him guilty and that the designation of the sentence lay completely with Olliver.

The trial went like clockwork.

The formalities over, the depositions of the witnesses were played from tapes, to the court and into the record. The first was that of a Captain of Police who was in charge of the police office at the airport. He testified that just before the arrival of the plane he had received a long distance telephone call from Chicago. The caller, a woman, had refused to give her name but had told him that a man named Crag, whom she described, would be a passenger on the plane and was carrying *nephthin*. He described detaining and searching Crag, and finding the drug. Then, on the tape, he was questioned by

Crag's attorney. Yes, he had tried to trace the Chicago call. They had found that it came from a public booth but found no clue or lead to the identity of the anonymous informant. Yes, the search had been perfectly legal. For such emergencies the airport police office kept on hand a supply of John Doe and Jane Doe warrants for detention and search. They were used whenever, in his judgment, use was indicated. In the case of a tip, anonymous or otherwise, a passenger was always detained and searched. No harm was done if the passenger was found innocent of contraband.

Three other members of the airport police detail told similar stories; all had been present at the search and testified that the *nephthin* had been in his possession. Crag's attorney had not questioned them.

Crag's own story came next. He had been permitted to tell it first in his own words and he described boarding the plane and finding his seat to be next to that of a man whom he described as tall, slender, well-dressed. There had been no conversation between them until the plane had neared Albuquerque, when the man had introduced himself as Zacharias and had claimed to be a cigarette salesman for a campany introducing a new brand of cigarettes. He had talked about the new brand and had pressed a package of them on Crag as a free sample. The man had left the plane hurriedly and was out of sight when the police had stopped Crag and had taken him to the airport police office to search him.

Following on the tape was Crag's questioning by the prosecuting attorney. He failed to change any detail of Crag's story, but Crag had been forced to hurt his own case by refusing to answer any questions whatever about himself aside from the brief episode he had just narrated.

Then, in refutation of Crag's story, the prosecution introduced the tape of one further witness, a man named Krable, who testified after being shown a picture of Crag, that he had sat next to him on the plane flight in question, that he had not introduced himself as Zacharias or under any other name, that there had been no conversation between them and that he had given Crag nothing. Questioning by the defense attorney only strengthened his story by bringing out the fact that he was a respectable businessman, owner of a men's haberdashery, that he had no criminal record and that his life was an open book.

There was further testimony from Crag after he had been confronted with Krable. He agreed that Krable was the man who had sat next to him, but stuck to his story that Krable had introduced himself as Zacharias and had given him the cigarette package.

That was all of the testimony. While Olliver was briefly charging the jury Crag smiled to himself at the simplicity and perfection of the frame-up. So few people need have been involved. No more than four. The tipster who had sent him to Albuquerque. A person in charge of seating arrangements to see that he sat where they wanted him to sit. A woman to make the anonymous phone call. And Krable, who was no doubt as respectable as he claimed to be and who had been chosen for that very reason, so that Crag's story would sound like a desperate invention—as it had sounded, even to Crag himself—in comparison to Krable's story. The only reason he hadn't pleaded guilty was that the plea would not have been accepted unless he'd followed through and told them where and how he'd obtained the *nephthin*—and the only way he could do that was the way he'd done.

The five members of the jury filed into the little jury room adjoining the court. They were back within minutes and their chairman reported a unanimous verdict—guilty.

Judge Olliver crisply ordered the courtroom cleared and the sound machines cut off. The trial itself was over. Sentence was always pronounced after the private conversation customary between judge and prisoner. The judge might announce his verdict immediately thereafter or take up to twenty-four hours to make his decision.

The trial, to Crag, had been a farce. This was it, and

he found himself growing tense. The courtroom was clear now, except for the two guards, the judge and himself.

"The prisoner will advance."

Crag walked forward and stood stiffly before the judge's desk, his face impassive.

"Guards, you may leave. Remain outside the door, please."

That was a surprise. True, a judge had the option of sending the guards outside or of having them remain, but he always had them remain when he felt that he was dealing with a dangerous man. At Crag's previous trial, despite the fact that the verdict had been an acquittal, Olliver had had the guards remain. Undoubtedly, then, Olliver had felt or recognized the savagery in Crag, had feared to provoke him to violence by the things he intended to say. That was understandable; under circumstances much more dangerous to himself, would he dismiss the guards?

Crag shrugged off the question. It didn't matter, and if Olliver delivered his verdict now and it was the psycher, he'd start his break from here, by killing Olliver. Then the two guards outside the door, and toward freedom as far as he could go before they shot him down.

He heard the door close behind the guards, and stood waiting, his eyes fixed on a point on the wall just over and behind Olliver's head. He knew well enough what Olliver looked like without looking at him. A big man, broad shouldered, with iron gray hair and a florid face that could be stern, as it was now and as it had been throughout the trial, or could be pleasant and winning, as it was when he made campaign speeches on television.

There was no doubt in Crag's mind which expression Olliver's face would be wearing now. Until Olliver said, "Look at me, Crag." and Crag looked down and saw that Olliver was smiling.

Olliver said softly, "Crag, how would you like your freedom, and a million dollars?"

And then, "Don't look at me like that, Crag. I'm not

joking. Pull up a chair, one of those comfortable jurors' chairs, not the one you've been sitting on, have a cigarette, and let's talk."

Crag got a chair and sat down in it, but warily. He accepted a cigarette gratefully; they weren't allowed in the cells. Then he said, "You talk. I'll listen."

Olliver said, "It's simple. I have a job I'd like you to do for me. I think you're one of the few men alive who might be able to do it. If you agree to try it, your freedom. If you succeed, the million. And maybe more if you want to keep on working with me after that.

"And it's not a racket, Crag. The opposite. A chance to help humanity, to help me help to lift it out of the bog of decadence into which it has fallen."

"Save that for your speeches, Judge. I'll settle for freedom and the million—if you're on the level. A question first. The charge against me was a frame-up. Yours? To put me in a spot where I'll have to work for you?"

Olliver shook his head. "No. But I'll admit that, when I saw on the docket that you were to be tried, I deliberately obtained permission to sit at the trial. Was it a frame-up?"

Crag nodded.

"I suspected so. The evidence against you was too pat, your story too thin. Any idea who *did* engineer it?"

Crag shrugged. "I have enemies. I'll find out."

"No," Olliver said sharply. "If you accept my proposition, you'll have to agree to let any private vengeance you have in mind go, until you've done my job first. Agreed?"

Crag nodded a bit sullenly, but he said, "Agreed. What's the job?"

"This isn't the time or place to tell you that. Since you've agreed in advance to do it, and since it will take some explaining, we'll talk about it after you're a free man."

"But if I decide it's too dangerous and turn it down?"

"I don't think you will. It's a difficult job, but I don't think you'll turn it down, for a million dollars. And there may be more for you in it than merely money. I'll take a chance that you won't turn it down. But let's get to brass tacks, about your escape."

"Escape? Can't you—" Crag stopped, realizing that the question he'd been about to ask was absurd.

"Escape, of course. You were judged guilty of a major crime and on strong evidence. If I were to free you, even to give you a light sentence, I'd be impeached. *I* have enemies too, Crag; any man in politics has."

"All right, how much can you help me toward an escape?"

"Arrangements are being made; when they are completed you'll be told what to do."

"Told how?"

"By the speaker in your cell. A—a friend of mine has access to the circuits. In fairness, I should tell you that we can't arrange any foolproof escape for you. We'll do what we can and you'll be on your own from there."

Crag grinned. "And if I'm not good enough to make it from there, I wouldn't be good enough to do the job you have for me outside. So you've nothing to lose if I'm killed escaping. All right. What sentence are you going to give me meanwhile?"

"It will be better if I announce that I'm taking the full twenty-four hours to decide. If, now, I sentence you to either Callisto or the psycher, preparations to send you to one or the other will start immediately. I don't know exactly how fast such preparations would proceed, so it's safer to keep the sentence in abeyance."

"Good. And after I escape?"

"Come to my house. Seven-nineteen Linden. Don't call. My phone is tapped, undoubtedly."

"The house is guarded?" Crag knew that the houses of most important political figures were.

"Yes, and I'm not going to tell the guards to let you in. They're members of my own party, but I wouldn't trust them that far. Getting past them is your problem. If you can't do that, without help or advice from me, you're not the man I think you are, or the man I want. But don't kill them unless you have to. I don't like violence." He frowned. "I don't like it, even when it's necessary and in a good cause."

Crag laughed. "I'll try not to kill your guards—even in a good cause."

Olliver's face flushed. He said. "It *is* a good cause, Crag—" He glanced quickly over his shoulder at the clock on the wall and then said, "All right, we've time left. I've often talked to a prisoner half an hour or longer before sentencing him."

"You talked to me that long last time before *freeing* me, after I was acquitted."

"And you know you had it coming. You *were* guilty—that time. But I started to tell you what the cause is, so you won't laugh at it. I'm starting a new political party, Crag, that's going to bring this world, the whole solar system, out of the degradation into which it has sunk.

"It's going to end bribery and corruption by taking us back to old-fashioned democracy. It's going to be a middle-of-the-road party that will end the deadlock between the Guilds and the Syndicates. Both of those parties—I'll face it; even the one I'm a member of—represent ridiculous extremes. The Guilds grew out of Communism and the Syndicates grew out of Fascism and between them something we once had and called Democracy got lost."

Crag said, "I see your point. Maybe I even agree. But are you going to get anywhere with it? Both the Guilds and Gildeds have made Democracy a swear word and a laughingstock. How can you get the public to accept it?"

Olliver smiled. "We won't call it that, of course. It's the *word* that's discredited, not the idea. We'll call ourselves the Cooperationists, represent ourselves as trying to steer a middle course between extremes. And half the members of each of the old parties, those who want honest government, are going to come to us. Yes, we're operating undercover now, but we'll come into the open before the next elections, and you'll see. Well, that's enough for now. Everything between us understood?"

Crag nodded.

"Good." Olliver pressed a button on the desk and the guards came in. As Crag left with them he heard Olliver, the sound machine turned on again, saying into it that he was postponing his decision on sentencing for twenty-four hours.

Back in his cell, he paced impatiently. Tried to think ahead. Did the plan for his escape—or chance at escape—include a change of clothes? He looked down at himself. The gray shirt might pass, if he opened it at the throat and rolled up the sleeves above his elbows. But the baggy gray trousers shrieked of prison. He'd have to take the trousers off a guard, and even they wouldn't be too good and he'd have to change them for shorts as soon as he had a chance. Almost all private citizens of Albuquerque wore shorts in summer.

He rolled up the sleeves and opened his collar, then stopped in front of the metal mirror set into the wall over the washstand and studied himself. Yes, from the waist up he'd do. Even the short haircut, since it was almost as common outside of prison as in.

And his face—he was lucky there, for it was a very ordinary face that looked neither vicious nor criminal, a face that didn't stand out in a crowd, a hard-to-remember face. He'd paid plenty for that face, to the same surgeon in Rio who'd taken care of the artificial hand for him. The face he'd been wearing before that had been becoming a bit too well known in the underworld, a more dangerous thing than being too well known to the police.

The body under that face was just as deceptive. Neither taller nor broader than average, it masked the wiry strength and endurance of an acrobat and it knew every clean and dirty trick of fighting. Crag could take an average man with one hand, his right, and often had, in fights before witnesses when he didn't want to give away the secret of his left hand. That was ace-in-the-hole, for emergencies. When he used it, he meant business.

He paced again, stopped to look out the window.

Thirty flights down to freedom. But only the top three levels were jail floors; if he got below them he could take an elevator from the twenty-seventh down and be comparatively safe.

But what were his chances of making those first three floors? Better than even, he guessed, with whatever help Olliver was going to give him. A thousand to one against him otherwise; that was how he'd guessed his odds before the trial.

Olliver, of all people! Turning out to be as big a crook as all the rest of the politicians after all. Aiding a criminal to escape so the criminal could steal something for him. Or could there be some truth in the story Olliver had handed him? Could Olliver really be acting from altruistic motives? Crag shrugged mentally. It didn't matter.

But Olliver had really surprised him. He wondered how his, Crag's, face must have looked when Olliver, instead of sentencing him, had smiled and asked him if he wanted freedom and a million.

Crag chuckled, and then suddenly was laughing aloud.

A woman's voice, amused, asked, "As funny as that, Crag?"

He looked quickly up at the grill in the ceiling. The voice said, "Yes, it's two-way now; you can answer back. Few people know it but any of the cell communicators can be used two ways. Sometimes the police want to listen in when a lawyer talks to his client. Even the police are crooked, Crag. Or do you already know that?"

"Are you using the communicator just to tell me that?"

"Don't be impatient, Crag. You have time to kill, and so do I. I took over this control cubicle from the guard on duty here by sending him on an errand. He'll be gone at least fifteen minutes."

Crag said, "You must be high brass to be able to do that."

"What I am doesn't matter, except that I'm helping

you. Not for your sake, Crag, but because you may be
able to help—you know whom. When the guard returns,
I'll come to you."

"You'll come here?"

"Yes, to bring you certain things you'll need for an
escape. While I'm here I'm going to activate the lock on
your door, so I can get in when I come. But do not leave
the cell now. In fact, you will not leave it for half an
hour after I have come and gone. Understood and
agreed?"

"Understood and agreed," Crag said. He heard a click
in the lock of his door.

"What things are you bringing?" Crag asked. But there
was no answer and he realized that the connection had
been broken.

He sat on the cot and waited. Why did it have to be a
woman who'd been assigned to help him? He hated
women, all women. And this one had dared to sound
amused, and condescending.

Then the door opened and the woman came in quickly and closed it. High brass, all right; her severe uniform
was of Chief Psycher Technician. Psycher technicians
were important people and there were only a few of
them. To become one, you had to have doctorate degrees in both psychology and electronics, plus a lot of
political pull. Well, if she was closely associated with
Olliver, the political pull was explained.

But she didn't look like a woman who would hold two
doctorates. She was beautiful. Not even the uniform
could conceal the soft curves of her body, nor could the
horn-rimmed glasses she wore or the fact that she was
completely without make-up conceal the beauty of her
face. Her eyes, even through faintly tinted glass, were the
darkest, deepest blue Crag had ever seen, and her hair,
what showed of it beneath the technician's beret, was
burnished copper. Crag hated her for being a woman
and for being beautiful, but mostly he hated her for
that hair; it was exactly the color Lea's hair had been.

Deliberately, to be rude, he remained sitting on the
cot. But if she noticed the rudeness she did not show it

in any way as she stood in front of him and opened her handbag. But her voice, now, was curt and business-like, with no trace of amusement or friendliness.

"The most important thing is this," she said. She tossed a little metal bar onto the cot beside him. "Carry it in a pocket. It's radioactive; without it or without a guard with you who has one, most of the portals here are death traps."

"I know," he said shortly.

A paper, folded small, was next. "A diagram showing a way out along which you're least likely to encounter guards. In case you do—"

A small heatgun was the next offering, but Crag shook his head at that. "Don't want it," he said. "Don't need it."

She put the gun back in her purse without protest, almost as though she had expected him to refuse it. Next, "A visitor's badge. It won't help you on the upper three levels—no visitors allowed here without a guard accompanying them—but once you're below that, it will keep the regular building guards from asking questions."

He took that. Next was a short paper-thin durium saw blade. "You'll use this to cut through the sliding bolt of your door. I'll lock it from the outside when I leave."

"Why?"

"Don't be stupid, Crag. That door can be locked from the outside, but it can be unlocked only from the control cubicle. And I just relieved the guard there. If your door is found unlocked, it will be known that only he or I could have released you. He would be more suspect than I, but I do not wish to draw even that much attention to myself."

"If you're being so careful," Crag said, "how do you know he's not listening in on our conversation now?"

"I don't know," she said calmly. "That is a chance I could not avoid taking. Now about clothes. I brought you shorts." From her purse she tosed a tight roll of silk onto the bed. "Couldn't bring shoes." She glanced down at his. "And those look like prison so I suggest you leave them. Civilians here wear sandals or go barefoot, about half and half, so you'll be less conspicuous barefoot than in shoes. I see you've had a thought about the shirt yourself, but I can improve it. I can leave you scissors, needle and thread; cut off the sleeves instead of rolling them. You can sew enough to baste a hem?"

"Yes." Crag hesitated. "But it would take me twenty minutes or so. I'd rather get going."

"You'll have time for that, for sawing the bolt, and for memorizing—and destroying—the diagram. All those together shouldn't take over forty minutes and forty minutes from now, on the hour, when you hear the clocks strike, will be the best timing for you. Don't leave until then even if you find yourself ready sooner."

"How about some money?"

"All right, here's twenty. You won't need more than that because you're to come to—you know where—as soon as you safely can. And sober."

Crag didn't bother to answer that. He never drank when he was working, or in danger. A criminal didn't live long if he drank at the wrong times.

"One more thing, Crag. You can fold the collar of that shirt so it looks more nearly like a sport shirt collar. Here, I'll—"

She reached for it and Crag jerked aside and stood up. "I'll take care of it," he said.

She laughed. "Afraid of me, Crag?"

"I don't like to be touched. Especially by a woman. Now if that's all, get out."

"Such gratitude, Crag. And about women—did anyone ever tell you you ought to be psyched, a little anyway? Well, at least you stood up for me, finally."

Crag didn't answer, and she turned and left. He thought she was still smiling. The lock of the door clicked again.

He wasted no time glaring at the door. He went to it quickly and started sawing at the bolt, venting his anger on the inanimate. He finished it and the other things he had to do long before the time allotted for them. He almost decided to leave right away, but re-considered and waited until he heard the clocks striking the hour.

He left quietly then and found the corridor empty. Followed it quickly and silently, left it when his mental picture of the diagram he had destroyed showed him where to turn. He went along a corridor and down a ramp. Just as he approached another corridor he heard the footsteps of two guards coming. He went back a few steps and stood in a recess in the wall, his left hand ready to strike if they came his way. But they went the other way at the turn and he went on. He came to the second ramp and made it safely. On this level he found more corridors, more portals, but no guards.

Then the final ramp, the one that took him to the twenty-seventh floor. Not far now—but surely there'd be a guard stationed at the final door or portal that led to the elevator hallway and relative safety.

▼▼▼▼▼▼▼▼▼▼▼▼▼▼▼▼▼▼▼▼▼▼▼▼▼▼▼▼▼▼▼▼▼▼

CHAPTER THREE

THERE was a guard. A quick look around the final turn showed him a closed door with a guard sitting in front of it. And he was awake and alert, although fortunately he did not happen to be looking straight ahead.

But he was awake and alert and with a heatgun unholstered and ready, held in his hand in his lap.

And on the wall over his head—

Crag smiled grimly as, back out of sight, he detached his left hand and got it ready to throw with his right. Either Olliver or the woman, or both, must have known what was on the wall over the guard's head—a small hemispherical blister that could only be a thermocouple set to give off an alarm at any sudden increase in temperature. Yet the woman had offered Crag a heatgun. It would have been suicide to shoot the guard with it. And if the guard had time to fire his own gun, even though it would be aimed away from the thermocouple, no doubt the rise in heat would be sufficient to set off the alarm anyway, even if he missed Crag. Not that he would miss, at ten feet or a bit less.

Nor would, nor did, Crag at that range. When he stepped out into sight his right hand was already drawn back to throw the missile, and it was in the air before the guard had time to more than start to lift the heatgun from his lap. Crag's hand hit him full in the face long before he had time to pull the trigger. And he'd never pull one again.

Crag walked to him and got his hand back, putting it on quickly as soon as he'd wiped the blood off it on the guard's uniform. Then he picked up the guard's gun, deliberately handling it by the barrel to get his prints on it, and deliberately bloodied the butt. They'd know who killed the guard anyway, and he'd rather have them wonder how he'd managed to take the guard's own

22

weapon away from him and kill him with it than have
them wonder, or perhaps guess, how he *had* killed the
guard. Whenever Crag killed with that left hand and
had time afterward he tried to leave evidence that some
other blunt weapon had been used.

Then, using the key that had hung from the guard's
belt, he went through the door and closed it behind him,
and no alarm operated. He could probably thank the
woman for that, anyway; without the radioactive bar
he'd have had a slim chance indeed. Yes, they'd given
him a fair chance—despite the fact that he'd also been
given a chance to spoil everything if he'd been stupid
enough to take that heatgun, and despite the fact that
she hadn't told him to get rid of that bar here and now
even though he knew, and she must have known, that
outside the sacred precincts of the jail those bars often
worked in reverse and set off alarms instead of stilling
them.

He got rid of his in a waste receptacle outside the
elevator bank before he pushed the button to summon
an elevator. A few minutes later he was safely on the
street, lost in the crowd and reasonably safe from pur-
suit.

The sidewalk was crowded with scantily clad people.
Save those in one or another kind of uniform, few if
any wore more than shorts or trunks, a sport shirt or a
T-shirt and sandals. Many men wore nothing above the
waist. So did a few women, mostly ones who had out-
standing good reasons for the extreme style. All of the
women who were barefoot and some of the men, had
gaudily painted toenails, usually gold or silver.

Vocoads blared in his ears. Eat at Stacey's, wear Try-
lon, visit the House of Strange Pleasures, use Cobb's
dentifrice, visit Madam Blaine's, drink Hotsy, use Safe
and be safe, travel Panam, buy, drink, visit, use, buy.

Crag ducked into a hotel and in the privacy of a
men's room booth he took off the gray prison shirt and
got rid of it down a waste disposal chute. Not because
the shirt itself would have been too likely to draw attention, not because he enjoyed semi-nudity, but be-

cause being shirtless made him look like a different man. The hard, flat musculature of his torso and shoulders made him look much bigger and at least twenty pounds heavier.

He broke the twenty-dollar bill to buy sandals at a little haberdashery shop off the hotel lobby and at a drugstore on the next corner he made two purchases: a cheap wrist watch—his own had been taken from him with his other possessions at the jail—that probably wouldn't run more than a few days but the band of which would cover the line where flesh met metal at his wrist, and a pair of sunglasses, which at least a third of the people on the streets were wearing. That was all he could do at the moment in the way of disguise, but it was enough. He doubted that even the prison guards who had been seeing him every day would recognize him now, certainly not from a casual glance or from passing him on the street.

Now, the sooner he got himself inside Olliver's house the less danger there'd be at that end. By now the guard's body would have been found and a check of cells would have been made. His escape was known and they were looking for him. They might well throw a protective cordon around the home of the judge who had presided at his trial. Escaped prisoners often hated their judges enough to attempt murder. True, in his case Olliver had deferred sentence, but all he had postponed was a choice between the two forms of maximum punishment he could deal out, so the police would logically reason that his deferring of that choice would not affect Crag's wish for vengeance, if he had such a wish.

They might also put men to guard the witnesses who had taped the testimony against him and there, in one case at least, they'd be justified. Crag had nothing against the airport police who had searched him and testified to finding the *nephthin,* for their testimony had been honest. But the man who had actually given him the drug and then had denied doing so was on Crag's list, although he could wait—and sweat—for a while, know-ing the police couldn't guard him forever. So was the tipster in Chicago who had sent him to Albuquerque on Crag's list. And before one of the two of them died, he'd tell Crag which one of his enemies had engineered the deal. But all that could wait and would have to wait. Men who are violent are seldom patient, but Crag was both.

But it was the other way around when it came to reaching Olliver; the sooner he made it the less danger there would be.

He took a cab and gave an address that would be two blocks away from the one Olliver had given him. Paid off the driver and pretended to push a doorbell and wait until the cab had turned a corner and was out of sight. Then slowly he strolled past Olliver's house, keeping to the opposite side of the street. There was a guard at the front door so there'd be one at the back, too; no use checking that. But as yet no extra guards were in sight, no cars parked nearby with men in them.

He strolled on past, considering what would be the best plan of action. Getting in by killing either guard would be simple. He need merely approach on the pretext of asking whether the judge was home, and then flick the man's chin with his left hand. It would be simple but useless if he wanted to be able to stay inside for what might be a long talk with Olliver. A dead guard, or even a missing one if he took the body inside with him, would be a dead giveaway. Armies of them would come in looking for him; they'd probably insist on searching, for Olliver's protection, even if Olliver tried to tell them that he wasn't there. They'd have warrants of course and he wouldn't be able to keep them out.

Getting down from the roof was a much better bet, if he could make the roof from the roof of the adjacent building, and he thought he could.

Olliver's home was three stories high and roughly cubical. It was sizeable enough, probably fifteen to twenty rooms, but quite plain and simple, externally at least. It was not the fashion for politicians who aspired to elective office to live ostentatiously, no matter how much money they had. If they loved luxury—and most of them did—they indulged that love in ways less publicly obvious than by living in mansions. The public believes what it thinks it sees.

The building next to Olliver's house was the same height and roughly the same shape, although it was an apartment building instead of a private home. Crag's casual look upward as he had passed had shown him that the roofs were level with one another and about fifteen feet apart. That building would be his best bet; the one on the other side of Olliver's home was also three stories, but it was too far away.

Out of sight from Olliver's house he crossed the street and strolled back toward it. He entered the adjacent building and looked over the inset mailboxes and buzzer buttons in the hallway. There were six apartments; obviously two on each floor, and numbers five and six would be on the top floor. The glass-fronted mailboxes for both of those apartments had names on them, but the box for apartment five, labeled Holzauer, was stuffed with what seemed like an undue quantity of mail for one day's delivery. Crag took from his pocket the visitor's badge he'd worn until he had left the Federation Building and used it to pick the lock of the mailbox. The Holzauers were away, all right; the letters in the box were postmarked various dates over a period of almost a week.

He closed and relocked the box and used the pin to let himself through the inner hallway door. He went up the stairs and used the same means to let himself into apartment five and to lock the door after him. Luckily, it was on the side of the building nearest the Olliver house.

He scouted the apartment first, and at leisure, since he'd already decided it would be better to wait until after dark to take his next step. Many people used the roofs by day for sunbathing and there was too much chance of someone on a nearby building seeing him if he tried the building-to-building jump in broad daylight.

He looked first for clothes, hoping to find a better-fitting pair of shorts—the ones that had been given him were a bit skimpy and tight-fitting—and a shirt to go with them. But he was not in luck there. Although he found clothing, he'd rather have gone naked than wear any of the garments he found. From the clothing, and from other evidence including a book shelf of very specialized pornography, it was obvious that Holzauer & Co. was a pair of homosexuals. Crag did not care for lace-trimmed panties or pink tulle jackets trimmed with leopard skin. But, with time to kill, he amused himself tearing them to shreds. And he began to hope, after glancing again at the pornography, that his unwitting hosts would return while he was there to greet them. But they didn't, and he contented himself with garnishing the pile of torn cloth with confetti from torn books. Crag did not like homosexuals.

No money, no jewelry. But that didn't matter, with a million-dollar job coming up. And Olliver would certainly advance him whatever money he'd need for expenses.

Time to start thinking, while it was still light, about what he'd be doing as soon as it was dark enough. He studied the Olliver house from one window, then another. There'd no doubt be a hatch door in the roof but if it was bolted from the inside, as most such doors were, there'd be no way he could open it from the outside, without special tools or without making noise. But on the third story one window was open at the top. Hanging from the edge of the roof, he'd be able to get in by way of that window.

While he was studying it out and measuring with his eye the distances involved, he heard cars stop out on the street and ran lightly to a window at the front corner of the apartment from which he could see what was going on.

There were two cars parked in front of the Olliver house. Five policemen got out of one car and four out of the other. They walked toward the house, two of them going around it to the back and the other seven going

to the front door. A man had remained in one of the
cars and as he put his head out of a window to call
something after the policeman, Crag saw that the man
was Olliver.

So that was why they hadn't immediately tripled or
quadrupled the guard on the house. They'd left it relatively unguarded, since Olliver had not been home as
yet. Now they'd escorted him home but were going to
search the house before he himself entered it. The house
would be a trap for Crag now, if he'd entered it right
away, by whatever means.

Had Olliver crossed him? Crag wondered for a moment, and then discarded the idea. What would Olliver
have had to gain by helping him escape if so soon afterward he had helped the police lay a trap to catch him?
No, this must have been an idea of the police, and Olliver must have been unable to dissuade them from giving
him what they considered maximum protection. Olliver
had no authority whatsoever over the police. Olliver
must be hoping right now that Crag had not yet entered,
or all of Olliver's trouble thus far would have been for
nothing.

Crag congratulated himself on not having made that
mistake.

Standing back far enough from the window not to be
observed, he waited and watched. After about twenty
minutes, ample time for that many men to have made a
thorough search of a building that size, the nine men
came out. Crag counted carefully to make sure no extra
guards had been left. There'd still be one man and only
one man at each of the two entrances.

Olliver got out of the car, talked to one of the policemen briefly, and then went to the front door of the
house—and inside, no doubt, although Crag couldn't see
the doorway from his window. The policemen got into
the cars and both cars started. One of the cars U-turned
and parked across the street and a few buildings away.
Suddenly there seemed to be no one in it; the driver
had used the control that activated the windows into
one-way glass. The car was unmarked as a police car and

from now on, to anyone walking or driving past, it would seem to be merely an empty car parked at the curb. The other car went on and turned the corner. But Crag knew it wouldn't really be leaving and got to a back window in time to see it park in the alley opposite the point where the other car parked in the street.

And from overhead came the drone of a helicopter. Crag listened long enough to make sure that it was circling the neighborhood and not just passing over, and swore to himself. That helicopter, with a good view of all the roofs in the block, would be a real obstacle to his entering by the route he'd planned to use.

But there was no use worrying about it now, since he did not plan in any case to make his entry before darkness fell, and by that time the situation might have changed. And a look at his wrist watch showed him that darkness was at least two hours away, so he decided that he might as well sleep for those two hours; it had been a big day and might, for all he knew, be the prelude to a bigger night. Or to no night at all, if he were discovered, for he was still determined that he would not be taken alive.

Crag had trained himself to be able to sleep on a minute's notice, any time and anywhere. Almost anywhere, that is; with a disgusted look at the oversized ornate bed of his hosts and a disgusted thought about the things that must have happened on it, he made himself comfortable in an armchair. And within a minute he was asleep, soundly but so lightly that the scrape of a key in the lock or any other sound that could indicate danger would have awakened him instantly.

No sound woke him, but the passage of an almost exact two hours did. He woke completely and suddenly, as a cat wakes. Stood and stretched, hearing the helicopter still circling overhead.

Quick looks out of two windows showed him that both of the police cars were parked as he had last seen them. And that, although it was fully dark, there was a bright moon. From the angle of shadows he determined that the moon was about halfway between the zenith and the horizon, and he wondered if he should wait until it had set, for moonless darkness. But that might make things even more dangerous. Without moonlight, the helicopter would be almost useless—even with a searchlight it could observe too small an area at a time —and they'd probably dispense with it and post men on Olliver's roof or on other roofs nearby. Right now, with the moon as bright as it was, they were probably depending upon it completely for watching roofs. It would be easier to fool one heli load of cops than an unknown number of watchers on roof tops.

Every helicopter had a blind spot, directly beneath itself. If it ever went straight over, instead of circling—

Crag groped on the dresser top and found a hand mirror and a nail file. In the living room he climbed the ladder to the roof hatch and pushed it ajar, propping it with the file. Watchers in the heli would think nothing of it being that way, if they noticed, for many top-floor dwellers so propped their hatches for ventilation on a warm evening. And the air, so soon after darkness, was still quite warm; probably there were dozens of raised hatches in the block. On evenings as warm as this, too, many people sat, or even slept, on their roof tops, and Crag used the mirror, held it at various angles, to check the roof tops in all directions. He saw no one and decided that those in the immediate neighborhood who might otherwise be using their roofs this evening were no doubt discouraged from doing so by the annoyance of having a heli so low and so continually overhead. If that was true, having the heli there might be more of an advantage than a disadvantage, and besides its constant drone would help to hide any slight sound he himself might make.

He put the mirror down flat on the roof and in it followed the motions of the heli as well as he could, for a long time. As nearly as he could judge, it was flying ninety or a hundred feet above the roof tops and holding the same altitude. Most of the time it flew in a circle the center of which was the Olliver residence and the radius of which was about half a block. But once in a while, either because the pilot wanted to vary the monotony or wanted to change his angle of observation, it would make a figure eight instead, with the Olliver roof dead center at the crossing at the center of the eight. Once in a while? Crag watched a while longer and counted; there was a figure eight after every fourth circle, and that meant the heli was on autopilot and that the pattern had been set deliberately and he could count on it.

And if, at one of those crossings directly overhead, he started at the exactly right instant, he'd have several seconds during which they wouldn't be able to see him at all, and if, at the end of that period he was hanging from the eaves of the roof opposite, he'd have a slightly longer period to get himself inside the open window while they turned and came back. It would take fast work and split-second timing. With his eye he measured the number of steps, six, he could take between the hatch and the edge of the roof, and decided it would be enough of a start for him to jump the fifteen feet. If it wasn't—well, he'd taken chances before.

He watched and timed three more figure eights until he could tell from the sound of the heli, coming from behind him, the exact moment when it was safe for him to start, and on the fourth he started.

And kept going. Dropped the hatch shut behind him, ran the six paces and jumped. Landed lightly and caught his balance only inches past the edge of the Olliver roof, took a step backwards and let himself drop, catching the edge of the roof with his right hand and holding. Got his feet through the open top half of the window and hooked the inside of the top of the frame with his metal left hand, and a second later was inside the window, silently and safely. A maneuver that only an acrobat, or Crag, could have made. Stood quietly inside the window listening to the heli until he was sure that it was continuing the pattern as before, that the pilot hadn't taken over from the autopilot to drop lower and hover to investigate any movement he might have seen.

He didn't think there'd be any guards inside the house,

but there might be servants, so he took no chances. He faced away from the moonlight and let his eyes become accustomed to the relative darkness of the room—a bedroom, but unoccupied—before he crossed it and found himself in a hallway that was even darker. He found the stairs and went down them silently. There were no lights on the second floor and he went down another flight. The first floor hallway was lighted dimly, but there was a crack of brighter light under a door across from the foot of the stairs.

He went to the door and stood in front of it, listening. Heard two voices, Olliver's and that of a woman, but the door was thick and he heard too faintly to make out what was being said.

The fact that there was a woman's voice, too, made him hesitate. But Olliver had told him to come and must be expecting him; if he had a woman with him now she must be someone in his confidence, as the Chief Psycher Technician had obviously been.

Crag opened the door and stepped boldly into the room.

Olliver was seated behind a massive mahogany desk. His eyes went wide and his jaw dropped when he saw Crag. He said, "My God, Crag, how did you make it? I never thought of them searching and then guarding this place, since I hadn't sentenced you. But they insisted on it. I thought you'd hide out and look me up a week or two from now."

But Crag's eyes, after a quick look at Olliver, had gone to the woman. She looked familiar but at first look he couldn't place her, might not have placed her at all if it had not been for the burnished copper hair, now no longer confined under a technician's beret, and for her voice: her eyes glinted with amusement as she looked at the man behind the desk and said, "I told you he'd come this evening, Olliver, and you laughed at me. Isn't it my turn to laugh now?" And she did laugh, a pleasing sound. "And, Olliver, don't ask the man how he did it. He won't tell you, and why should you care?"

She was unbelievably beautiful. The costume of a

technician had not completely hidden the fact that she
had a beautiful body, but the costume she wore now
flaunted the fact. In the bare-midriffed evening style,
there was only a wisp of almost transparent material
above her waist. The skirt was long and opaque, but
before it flared at the knees it molded her hips and
thighs by fitting her as a sheath fits a sword. Her face,
now with subtle makeup and unmasked by glasses, was
worthy of the blazing glory of the copper hair that
framed it. She smiled at Crag, and her eyes danced, then
very deliberately and very slowly her eyes went down
him to his sandals and back again. She said, "Who would
have guessed, seeing you in those prison clothes?" It
was so frankly and so semi-humorously done that no
man could have resented it.

Except Crag. He glared at her and then turned to
Olliver. "Does this woman have to be here while we
talk?"

Olliver had recovered his poise, and smiled. "I'm
afraid she must be here, Crag. She's very important to
my plans, our plans. But I'd better introduce you. Crag,
this is Judeth. My wife."

Crag growled. "If she's got to stay, give me something
to put on. I won't be looked at that way."

Olliver's face stiffened a bit but he said, "There are
robes in that closet. But you're being ridiculous, Crag.
These are not Victorian times. This is the twenty-third
century."

Wordlessly Crag stalked to the closet and opened it.
Several houserobes hung there and Crag grabbed at
random a maroon silk one. He put it on, realizing too
late, after he'd closed the closet door, that the robe must
be Judeth's, not Olliver's; the shoulders fitted snugly
and the sleeves were a trifle short, whereas Olliver had
massive shoulders and long arms. But he realized by
now that he'd already been a bit ridiculous and it would
have made him seem more so to go back to the closet
now and change robes. After all, houserobes were worn
by both men and women and this was a plain one, although of beautiful material. Still—

"It won't contaminate you, Crag," Judeth said.

But he could keep his dignity only by ignoring that. And by, henceforth, ignoring *her*, and everything she said and did, insofar as possible. Either that or, if Olliver insisted on keeping her around, walking out on Olliver and a chance to make a million dollars. And a million dollars was real moolah, nothing to be taken lightly.

"Sit down, Crag," Olliver said.

He saw that Olliver had already sat down behind his desk and that Judeth had perched herself on a corner of it and was now looking at him quite seriously, not at all mockingly.

Crag seated himself stiffly. in a straight chair, turning to face Olliver and not his wife. "One question," he said. "You really meant it this afternoon? And you have the million?"

Olliver nodded. "I really meant it. And I have most of the million now and will have the rest before you finish the job; it's nothing you can do overnight, and it's on Mars. Not my own money, you understand; it's a fund being raised by—"

Crag waved that aside. "I don't care whose it is as long as it will be mine if I do the job for you. And the sooner I start, the better. I got in here tonight and I can get out tonight. Tell me what the job is, give me expense money. I'll be on my way."

Olliver shook his head slowly. "I'm afraid it's not that simple, Crag. You see, to do this job you'll have to go to the psycher first."

CHAPTER FOUR

IF CRAG's mental reflexes had not been fully at fast as his physical ones, Olliver would have died in the next second. As it was, he came within six inches of dying; that was how far from his head Crag's hand—his left hand—stopped. Had that blow been completed, the woman would have died a fraction of a second later. Crag had taken the three steps that took him to the desk so fast one might have thought he blurred.

Two things saved them. One was the fact that Olliver's hands were in plain sight on the desk, nowhere near a push button or an open drawer. The other, the fact that the thought had time to flash across Crag's mind that it did not make sense for Olliver to have meant what he said. Psyching would make Crag's talents and skills useless for Olliver's purpose, whatever it was.

Judeth's voice was tense. "Wait, Crag." Out of the corner of his eye, Crag could see that she had not moved, was not moving, a muscle. Even her eyes were looking, not at him but at where he had been sitting. "As you have already seen, or we'd be dead by now, he did not mean that."

Olliver's handsome face was no longer florid, and his voice was hoarse. "All I meant was that—"

The woman's voice cut across his, sharply. "Be quiet, Ollie, and let me explain. That was incredibly stupid. I told you that Crag—" She broke off and her voice changed, becoming carefully impersonal. "Crag, will you sit down and let me explain? I promise you neither of us will move. Ollie, keep your hands as they are, exactly. And your mouth shut. Agreed, Crag?"

Crag didn't answer, but he backed away to the chair, watching both of them carefully. He sat gingerly on the edge of it; he'd be even faster this time if Olliver moved.

Judeth said, "As you realized in time, Crag, you

35

would be useless to us psyched. But you'd be almost equally useless to us as a hunted criminal. Do you see that?"

"I've been hunted before," Crag said. "And by people more dangerous than the police."

"True, but this is a very special and difficult job. And besides, Olliver promised you your freedom. That meant your full freedom, not as a hunted man."

"You mean a faked psycher certificate."

"Of course. A start from scratch, a clean slate. Without even your underworld enemies interested in you."

"It can't be done," Crag said. "It's been tried before."

"Because it was only a forged certificate, not a genuine one fully backed by all the facts and records. The difference is that you really will have gone to the psycher—but without being psyched. It's foolproof." She moved, for the first time, to turn her head and look at Olliver. Scorn came into her voice. "Even against a fool like my husband here, who so nearly got both of us killed a moment ago."

Crag's mind was working furiously. It seemed too simple, too perfect. He said—although he himself saw a simpler answer to the problem—"I'll have to let myself be recaptured. What if the police shoot first and capture afterwards?"

"Because you'll be captured here and now, when we've finished talking. Olliver can have a gun on you when we call the police in from outside. You'll already be captured and they'll have no possible excuse for shooting."

Crag nodded. "And you would handle the—psyching?"

"Of course. No chance of a slip-up there. I'm the only technician there right now; my assistant is on vacation. The timing is perfect. Any more questions?"

"Yes." Crag looked at her, his eyes hard. "How do I know that I can trust you?

Her eyes met his unwaveringly. "You can, Crag. I can see why you doubt, and—I'm sorry. I should have known better than to tease you, to make you self-conscious, a few minutes ago. I apologize."

"And you promise, under the psycher, to do nothing whatever to my mind?"

"I do. Think, and you'll know I wouldn't want to. It would make you useless to us. And if I even tried to change one little thing, you'd kill me afterwards. I know that."

"If you erased the memory that you'd changed it?"

"You know better than that, Crag. The process is not that selective. I'd have to erase all your memories or none. Otherwise we'd take away only a man's experiences and the things that led to them, and leave him the rest of himself. Someday we may be able to do that, but not as yet."

Crag nodded again. And this time Olliver, his face no longer pale, said, "Well, Crag?"

"All right. Get your gun."

Olliver slid open a drawer. "Put that robe back where you got it. Might be a little hard to explain."

"Wait. Why did we have to go through all this? Why couldn't you have explained this to me at your private talk after the trial. You could have sentenced me to the psycher then. Why the escape and recapture?"

Judeth said, "You wouldn't have believed him, Crag. You might have thought it was something he told to all the boys, to get them to go to the psycher happily. Or whatever you thought, you wouldn't have trusted him. The fact that we *did* help you escape takes care of that. We could have no possible motive for doing that and then sending you back to the psycher."

It made sense. Crag wouldn't have believed Olliver, then, to the extent of going to the psycher willingly. He'd have tried to escape, without help, before he'd have trusted anyone that far.

He stood up, reached to take off the robe and hesitated.

Judeth didn't laugh or mock him this time. She slid down from the desk and went toward the door. "I'll go for the police," she said. "Be ready."

Crag quickly hung up the robe and backed against the wall. He was standing there with his hands raised, Olli-

ver holding a gun on him across the desk, when the
police came in.

Nothing untoward happened on the way to the jail,
but something unpleasant happened after six guards
took him over from the police and took him to a cell.
They beat him into insensibility before they left him
there. But common sense and self-preservation made him
take it without fighting back. There were six of them
and each was armed with a heatgun besides the rubber
truncheon he was using. Crag might have killed three
or four of them but the chances were a thousand to
one against his getting them all before dying himself.
Those odds weren't good enough now; he'd have taken
them gladly if the alternative had been a real trip to
the psycher.

Consciousness returned to him in the middle of the
night and, every muscle in his body aching, he managed
to get from the floor to his cot. After a while he slept.

In the morning the speaker in the ceiling of his cell
woke him with the news that sentence had been pronounced on him and that guards would come to take
him to the psycher in half an hour. He sat up on the
edge of the cot painfully. He was naked; the guards had
stripped him the night before. But they had left prison
clothes in a corner of the cell and he put them on.

Six other guards came for him, ten minutes early so
they'd have time to beat him again. Less severely than
the previous beating because they didn't want him to lose
consciousness, and mostly about the arms and shoulders
because they wanted him to be able to walk. When a
buzzer sounded they took him to the psycher room
one floor down and strapped him into the chair. They
slapped his face a bit and one of them gave him a farewell blow in the stomach that made him glad he'd been
given no breakfast, and then they left.

A few minutes later Judeth came in. Again she was
dressed in uniform, as he had seen her the first time.
But now her beauty showed through even more for, after
having seen her as she'd been the evening before, he
knew every curve that the tailored uniform tried to hide.

She wore the tinted horn-rimmed glasses as she came in, but took them off as soon as she was inside.

Craig said nothing when she stood in front of him, looking down into his face.

She smiled slightly. "Don't look so worried. Crag. I'm not going to psych you. I'm not going to touch your mind in any way. I'm not even going to connect the electrodes."

He said nothing.

Her smile faded. "You know, Crag, I'd hate to adjust you, even if this was a straight deal. You're such a magnificent brute that I like you better the way you are than if you were a mild-mannered clerk or elevator operator. And that's what I could make you into—but I won't."

"Unstrap me," Crag said.

"With the door locked, and with us alone?" At his answering growl she smiled. "Oh, I'm not being femininely coy, Crag. I know how you hate women. But I also know your temper and I know how you've probably been treated since last night. With you free I'd have to watch every word I said to keep you from slapping me down—left-handed."

"You know about that?"

"I know more about you than you think. But I'm going to have to know a lot more. You're going to have to tell me a number of things about yourself."

"Why?"

"Because I'm going to have to turn in a report, of course. Including a case history, and a list of all major crimes to which you're supposed to be confessing right now under the machine. And that reminds me, I'd better turn it on." She went around the chair out of Crag's sight and a moment later a humming sound filed the room. Her voice said, "That's audible in the corridor outside and I don't want anyone to pass and notice that it isn't on by now. Don't worry; it's not connected to you in any way."

When she came into his sight again she was carrying a pad of paper and a stylus; she pulled up a chair this time and sat down in front of him, poising the stylus. "When and where were you born, Crag?"

"Make up your own story."

"Crag, this report will be checked against whatever facts are already known and recorded about you. If it doesn't hold up in every way, it will be obvious that this little séance was faked. There'll be an investigation at to why the machine failed to work properly on you. You'll be rearrested and brought back here—and *I* won't be the one operating the machine. I'll be in jail—or possibly even be sent to the psycher myself. To my knowledge, the crime that I'm committing right now has never been committed before and I don't know what my penalty would be. But there's no doubt about yours.

"I can't take any more chances than I'm already taking, so you *must* cooperate, or else. Or else I connect these electrodes right now and do the job honestly. I have no other choice. Do you understand that?"

"All right," Crag said grimly. "Go ahead."

"When and where were you born?"

Crag told her. And answered other routine questions. Through his graduation from space school, his early years as a spaceman.

"And your career as a spaceman ended when you lost your hand. Tell me about that."

"I'd been a spaceman seven years, and I was lieutenant on the Vega III. On Earth at the time; we were readying the ship for a Mars run. It was a pure accident —not my fault or anyone else's. Just one of those things that happen. Mechanical failure in a rocket tube set it off while I was cleaning it."

"But they blamed you?"

"Not exactly, but they sprang a technicality on me and used it to keep me from getting the compensation I was entitled to. Not only that, but took away my license and rank, turned me from a spaceman into a one-handed bum."

"What was the technicality?"

"Test for alcohol. It showed a minute quantity. I'd had a farewell drink—just one and a weak one—with a friend six hours before. But there happened to be witnesses and they were able to prove it *was* six hours before. The rule is, no drinks for eight hours before blast-off, and our schedule called for blast-off one hour after the accident happened. That put me technically in the wrong by exactly one hour. They used that fact to save themselves a lot of money. There was nothing I could do about it."

"And after that?"

"Oh, I got kicked around a while. Then I started kicking back. Is this going to take much longer?"

"Another hour, to make it take as much time as a real psyching would."

"These straps are getting to hurt. Will you let me out of this chair if I give you my parole?"

Judeth hesitated. Then she said, "In a minute, yes. But there's one thing that will have to go in my report that you might resent my questioning you about. I'd rather get it over first. Why do you hate women so much?"

"A pleasure to tell you. I'd been married about a month at the time of my accident, to a girl I was mad about. Do I have to tell you what she did when she learned I was short a hand and a job?"

"Divorced you?"

"She was remarried before I got out of the hospital."

"Did you ever—do anything about it?"

"You mean kill her? I hated her too much ever to want to see or touch her again—even to kill her."

"And you won't admit to yourself that you're still in love with her?"

Crag's face turned red and his veins swelled with sudden anger as he strained against the straps. "If I were free, I'd—"

"Of course you would. Anything more you want to tell me about her, Crag?"

"She had hair just the color of yours. And she was as beautiful as you." He paused a second. "No, you are more beautiful. And more evil."

"Not evil, Crag. Just ruthless. Like you. All right, that's enough about that, for my report. We won't mention her, or women, again. And all right, I'll release you now."

She unfastened the strap buckles and Crag stood up, first rubbing his forehead—the strap that had held his head back had been the most uncomfortable—and then his wrists. "What else?" he asked.

"List of crimes, for one thing. They want that particularly, so they can be written off as solved crimes instead of carried as unsolved ones. Might as well be honest about it. You've nothing to lose and it might as well sound good."

Crag laughed. "Get ready for a lot of writing."

"You can talk it into a sound recorder for the police to transcribe later. But before I turn it on—keep your voice flat and emotionless, talk as though you were in a trance. That's the way you'd sound if you were giving this information under the machine. And sit down again so you'll be the right distance from the pickup. Ready?"

Crag said he was ready. She clicked on the recorder.

Crag described briefly the major crimes he had committed, leaving out only two, jobs on which he had used accomplices who were still, as far as he knew, living. Then he looked at Judeth and gestured, and she shut off the machine.

"How about the crime I was convicted for, the *nephthin* job. Am I supposed to confess to that too?"

"I think you'd better, Crag. If I had to report that you didn't, it might stir up further investigation, and that's the last thing we want. Let's see, you were on Venus a year ago?"

"Yes."

"Say you bought the *nephthin* then, from a man whom you knew as—make up any name and a few details they can't check as to where and how you knew him. Say you'd held it until now, until you heard the price was high in Albuquerque, but that you had no special buyer in mind, you intended to look for one."

Crag nodded and added that to the list when she turned on the machine again. "Anything else?" he asked, when the recorder was off again.

"Yes, your escape yesterday. You'll have to tell how that was worked. I've worked out a story for you that can't be disproved."

"What is it?"

"The guard you killed on your way out was named Koster. Up to a year ago he was a bartender in Chicago. Say you got to know him there. Say he came to you day before yesterday in your cell and offered to help you escape for ten thousand dollars you could pay him after you were free. You accepted, and he gave you the things you needed for the escape."

"And why would I have killed him then?"

"To save ten thousand dollars."

"No, I wouldn't have had to pay it anyway if I hadn't wanted to. This is better. He gave me a route and a time which would take me through the portal he was guarding. He'd never intended really to help me escape; he intended to kill me and get credit for stopping an escape, and get promotion. But he was a little slow pulling his gun, as I was watching for just that particular double-cross, and I got the gun away from him and killed him with it."

"Much better. Tell it that way. You think fast, Crag."

She turned on the recorder again long enough for him to tell how he had escaped.

"All right," she said when she'd shut it off. "That finished things. The psycher, right now, is supposed to be expunging from your memory everything that, under its first cycle, you told me about yourself and your crimes." She looked at her watch. "We've got about another fifteen minutes. Better let me strap you in the chair again now."

"Why?"

"You're supposed still to be strapped in when I leave and the guards come for you. And when they loosen the straps there'd better be marks from them, especially the one across your forehead. Otherwise, they'll wonder."

He bent down and fastened the straps on his own ankles, then leaned back with his arms on the arms of the chair and let her adjust the others. The one on his left wrist reminded him. "You knew about my hand," he said. "How many others know? Does that go in the report? They might want to insist on my getting a regular one."

"Don't worry, Crag. No one else knows, unless it's Olliver. From the way you raised your left hand to strike him last night, I guessed that it was weighted. I didn't mention it even to him and I don't know if he made the same deduction or not."

"Good. Since we've time to kill, how about telling me what the job is that Olliver wants me to do?"

Judeth shook her head. "He wants to explain it to you himself. Besides, I've something more important to brief you on. I've got to tell you how to act after I leave you."

"I know. Meek like a rabbit."

"I don't mean that. First, you're supposed to be unconscious when I leave you here. The guards come here and unstrap you, and—"

"Give me another beating in the process?"

"No. You're no longer the person who killed one of them and they have nothing against you. You're starting fresh, Crag. They put you on a stretcher and take you by elevator to a hospital room on the twentieth level. They'll put you on a bed there and leave you to come out of it."

"How long am I supposed to be unconscious?"

"At least an hour. Some of them take longer."

"And then?"

"Pretend to wake up, and be confused. Remember, you don't know who you are or how you got there. Sit on the edge of the bed a while, as though you're trying to orient yourself."

"And then?"

"You'll get instructions. A nurse will be keeping an eye on you from time to time through the door. When she sees you're awake, she'll take you to see someone who'll explain things to you and tell you what to do."

"And what attitude do I take?"

"You're puzzled, and it's all right for you to ask ques-

tions. But be polite. Accept and follow whatever suggestions he makes. You'll be all right from there."

"But when and how shall I get in touch with Olliver?"

"Don't worry about it. That will be taken care of.
The less you know what to expect afterward the more
naturally you'll be able to act the role. Just remember
to watch your tongue—and your temper—every minute.
Every second.

"All right. Crag—be careful. Now pretend uncon-
sciousness. Close your eyes and breathe deeply and
slowly."

Distrustful of women as he was, Crag might have expected it, but he didn't. So the kiss on his lips jarred him
when it happened.

But he sat rigidly, not moving and not speaking, hating
her so greatly that he would not give her the satisfaction
of being cursed at, as she no doubt expected. Sat rigidly
while he heard her walk to the main switch of the psycher machine and shut it off. Heard her, in the deep
silence left by the sudden stoppage of the humming of
the machine, walk to the door, open and close it.

Only when, minutes later, he heard footsteps approaching the door did he remember to force himself
to slump into relaxation and breathe slowly and deeply.

By their footsteps and by the way they handled him,
he could tell that there were only two guards this time.
They weren't afraid of him any more, and they didn't
beat him. They lifted him out of the chair and onto a
stretcher. He was carried for a while, felt the sensation
of an elevator descent, was carried again and then rolled
from the stretcher onto a bed.

"The one that killed Koster," he heard one of the
guards say to the other. "Shall we give him something to
remember us by?"

"Nah," the other voice said. "What's the use? He ain't
the same guy now. Even if he felt it he wouldn't know
what it was for."

"Yeah, but—"

"Come on. Remember what's on tonight. Save your strength."

He heard them leave.

Already the psyching he was supposed to have had was beginning to pay off. He wondered how he was going to judge time—they'd taken his wrist watch, of course, along with his other possessions—until he heard a clock strike. That made it simple; all he had to do was wait until he heard it strike the next hour and it would be time for him to come back to consciousness.

Because of the pain in his muscles from the two beatings he'd had, it was hard to lie motionless that long, but Crag forced himself to do it. He opened his eyes then and as soon as he was sure he was alone in the room sat up on the edge of the bed. He was rubbing his shoulders gently when suddenly there was a nurse standing in the doorway.

"Feeling better?" she asked brightly.

Crag stood up, and winced. "I'm sore all over," he said. "What happened? Was I in an accident? How'd I get here?"

She smiled. "Everything's all right—and it'll all be explained to you. Or would you rather lie down again and rest some more first?"

He made his voice hesitant. "I'm—okay, I guess." He looked down at himself and pretended to be surprised. "Aren't these—prison clothes? Am I—?"

"Everything's all right. You're ready to leave as soon as things have been explained to you. And as for clothes—" She came on into the room and opened the door of a small closet. A shirt and slacks hung on hangers and a pair of sandals was on the floor under them. "—these are what you're to wear. If you want any help changing—"

"No," Crag said firmly. "But if there's a shower I could use, it might help this soreness."

She nodded and pointed to another door. "Right in there. You're sure you don't want help, for anything?"

Crag told her that he was sure, and waited until she

had left. Then he closed the door to the hallway and took a long shower, first as hot as he could stand it and then cold. Then he put on the clothes that had been provided for him, then opened the door to the hallway and looked out, pretending uncertainty.

The nurse was seated at a desk a dozen paces down the corridor. She had heard his door open and had looked up. She smiled again and beckoned and Crag walked over to the desk.

"Feeling better?" she asked. "You're looking *much* better."

"Feeling fine," Crag told her. "But I've been trying to remember things, and I can't even remember who I am or—anything."

"Don't worry. Everything is all right. I'll take you to Dr. Gray now."

She stood up and moved down the hall and Crag followed her. She showed him into a small waiting room and told him the doctor would see him in a few minutes. And in a few minutes a man with a round moon face opened an inner door and said, "Come in, Crag." Crag followed him into the office and took the offered chair.

He said, "You called me Crag. Is that my name, Doctor?"

"Yes. Will you have a cigarette, Crag?" Crag took one from the offered package, and the doctor leaned across the desk and held a lighter for him.

"Your name is Crag," he said, "unless you decide you want to change it. That will be your privilege if you so decide, after you've oriented yourself. You see, Crag, you were a criminal and—to make you able to fit into society—it was necessary that your memory of yourself and of your crimes be erased from your mind."

"What kind of a criminal was I? What did I do?"

"It's better that I don't answer that question for you, Crag. You should concentrate on the future and not on the past. Especially now, since the past no longer matters. Whatever crimes you committed are now off the books, forgotten. And you need feel no guilt for them because *you* are not the person who committed them, not any longer. You have a fresh start and you owe society nothing."

Crag nodded. "I see, Doctor."

The moonfaced man glanced at a card on the desk before him. "In one way you are fortunate. You have no living relatives, so there are no ties with the past whatsoever. In such cases, there are sometimes complications. But—" He cleared his throat and abandoned the sentence. "In another way, too, you are fortunate. You have a sponsor who offers you a much better and better paying job than most of our—ah—graduates start with. You will be a space pilot."

"Space pilot?" Crag didn't have to pretend surprise at that. Maybe there was a bit too much surprise in his reaction, for the doctor looked at him sharply.

"Yes," he said, "for a private craft. You're qualified; you had an A-rating license once. It was revoked, but reinstatement of any such license is automatic for any man who has gone through the psyching process. Unless the revocation was for incompetence, and yours wasn't. You'll take a short refresher course, naturally."

"What kind of a craft is it?"

"Four passenger, semi-atomic Class J-14. And your employer, Crag, is a great man, a great man indeed. His name is Olliver and he is possibly the greatest statesman in the system. At least in my opinion. But you may feel very fortunate that he took an interest in you and applied for your services. Otherwise you'd have had to start your new life as—well, in one of the menial categories. We always have more applications for such employees than we can fill. But of course if you don't want to go into space again, you're perfectly free to choose. You're a free man, Crag. You're being offered that job, not ordered to take it."

"I'll take it," Crag said. And remembered to add, "Thanks. Thanks very much."

The moon face smiled meaninglessly. "Don't thank me, thank Judge Olliver. You'll have a room and your meals at his house, incidentally, so you won't have to worry about looking for quarters. Here is his address, and ten dollars." He handed a slip of paper and a bill across the desk. "Cab fare, unless you'd rather walk. No hurry about when you get there."

Crag stood up, put both pieces of paper into his pocket, and thanked the doctor again.

Five minutes later, on the crowded sidewalk in front of the Judicial Building, he took a deep breath. He was *free*.

And hungry, damned hungry. It wasn't quite noon yet, but he'd already missed two meals in a row. Dinner last night because of his escape and recapture. Breakfast this morning, no doubt because for physiological reasons one was supposed to be psyched on an empty stomach. Either that or the guards had deliberately not fed him for the same reason they'd given him the beatings.

Also he wanted a drink, several drinks. But ten dollars wouldn't buy much of the kinds of liquor he wanted, whereas it would buy as big a lunch as he could eat, and one that would be a real contrast to the soggy synthetics that made up the bulk of prison fare. So lunch, at the best restaurant he could find, won.

Afterwards, replete, he wanted a drink worse than before, and sat for a while thinking of ways of raising a hundred or so for a binge before reporting to Olliver. But even the best of them involved a slight risk and was a risk worth taking now? He decided that it wasn't; he could wait, at least until he learned the score.

But still he was in no hurry to get to Olliver's, so he rang for his waitress and asked her to bring the latest newstab with a second coffee.

The newstab carried mention of his having been sentenced to the psycher but no details were given. They never were, on a psyching sentence; the legal theory was that a psyched man was entitled to a fresh start from scratch with everything against him, even fingerprint records, destroyed. Since he himself had forgotten his identity and his crime, society was required to do no less.

He leafed through the rest of the newstab. There was

nothing in it of interest to him. The usual politics and other crap.

Suddenly he wanted to walk, to savor his freedom. And, as well, it would be good for his muscles sore from the beatings. He paid his bill and left.

He took a roundabout course to Olliver's, partly to make the walk longer and partly to avoid the Martian Quarter, the spacemen's vice district. Too easy to get into trouble there, and much as he enjoyed trouble, this wasn't the time for it.

He walked fast, but with the catlike grace and easy balance of one used to a dozen variations of gravity. He thought about a million dollars.

A cool million dollars for one job.

The doorman at Olliver's front door was an ugly, a surly sadist, as were most guards, but he nodded politely to Crag and opened the door for him, told him the judge was waiting for him in the study. Crag followed the hall and let himself into the room he'd been in the evening before. He was glad to see Olliver was alone, again seated behind the massive desk.

Olliver said, "Sit down, Crag. You took your time getting here."

Crag didn't answer. "You've eaten?" Olliver asked, and Crag nodded.

"Good. Then we can talk. You *do* talk, don't you?"

"When necessary," Crag said. "Right now, I'd rather listen."

"All right. They told you you were being offered a job as my private pilot, and I presume you accepted."

"Yes."

"You can operate a J-14?"

"With a day or so to study the manual on it and familiarize myself with the controls."

"Good. You'll have a week before we take off for Mars. It's in Berth Ninety-six at the Port, and you can take as much time as you need to check yourself out on it. I can pilot it myself, but I never go into space without someone who can relieve me."

"And after we get to Mars?"

"You'll quit your nominal job and start on your real one. I'll tell you about it enroute; we'll have plenty of time."

"For the details, if you want to wait till then. But you can give me a general idea now. Maybe it's something I don't want to do, or think I can't do. Even for the price you offer I'm not taking on any suicide job. If I'm going to turn it down, it might as well be now."

"It's dangerous, but not that dangerous. I think you'll try it. I'll gamble that you will; you can still turn it down after we reach Mars."

"I'll wait for the details, but I still want to know the general nature of the job. Maybe I'll be wanting to make preparations even this coming week. Maybe there'll be something I'll want to get for the job that I can get on Earth more easily than on Mars."

"All right, I see your point on that. I suppose it might save time later to let you start planning as soon as possible. In fact, if you'll agree definitely to accept or decline the job now, I'll tell you everything about it right now—except one thing, and you can decide without knowing that."

"All right, go ahead."

"I want you to steal a certain object from Menlo."

Crag whistled softly. "Practically a fortress," he said.

"Yes, but not impregnable to someone taking a job as a guard to get inside it. And that's where your psycher certificate is important. Men otherwise qualified and with recent psycher certificates are *known* to be honest, are much more readily hired as guards than anyone else, no matter what they were before. In fact, no one even cares what they were before, and some of them never ask so you can safely deny that you know your former identity."

Crag smiled grimly. "And if there aren't any openings, I can waylay a guard in town and make one."

"Won't be necessary. Menlo is isolated and Eisen doesn't allow any women there. For those two reasons

Eisen has to pay a premium price to get employees, and even so has quite a turnover You'll have no trouble getting a job."

"And this object I'm to steal—is it easily portable?"

"You can carry it in a pocket."

"Menlo's a big place. Will you be able to tell me where to look for this object?"

"Yes, but not how to get it."

"Has anyone else made a previous attempt to get it?"

"Yes. I—we had a spy in Menlo, Crag, six months ago. As a technician, not a guard. He helped Eisen work on this—object, and told me about it. I ordered him to try to get it, made him the same offer I'm making you. A few weeks later I read a report that he'd been killed accidentally. Whether that was true or whether he was caught and privately executed or not, I don't know."

"Probably sprang a deathtrap. I've heard Menlo is full of them."

Olliver shrugged. "He wasn't a professional criminal. Not in your league at all. I should have been satisfied with using him as a source of information and not have expected more of him. But ever since then I've been looking for the right man for the job—until I saw your name on the docket a week ago and applied for jurisdiction. Well, Crag?"

"That's all there is to it? I obtain this object and give it to you?"

"One other thing, if possible. You're good with tools, aren't you?"

"Yes. If a guard job won't get me close enough I can probably get myself into the machine shop."

"Might help. But it wasn't what I had in mind in asking you. If you can possibly fabricate a dummy duplicate of the object and leave it in place of the real one, it will help. The object will be worth much more to us if Eisen doesn't know it's missing. But I'll settle for your getting it, under any circumstances."

"How many people aside from yourself and Eisen know of the existence of this object, and its value?"

"No one, to my knowledge, outside Menlo. And prob-

ably not very many there. That's as to its existence.
Crag. As to its value, I don't believe anyone—not even
Eisen himself—knows that, besides me. It's an invention
of his which he thinks is impractical and almost worthless. But *I* see in it a possibility for making billions of
dollars—and billions of dollars is what the Cooperation-
ist Party is going to need before it comes out into the
open against the two established parties." Olliver paused
and then asked again, "Well, Crag?"

"One more question. Have you got a million dollars,
in cash? Or am I supposed to wait for a pay-off out of
hypothetical billions?"

"The million is in cash. Not my own personal funds,
but in the war chest of the party. My collaborators in
the party know only that I know a way to invest that
million—which would be a drop in the bucket for
launching a new political party—in such a way as to
bring in all the money we'll need. They have agreed to
trust me to do so, without knowing how. As head of the
party and its future candidate for system coordinator,
they've given me carte blanche in the disbursement of
party funds. If I could tell you who was associated with
me in this, Crag, you'd realize what a big thing it is."

"I don't care about that," Crag said. "The million's in
cash and in your hands. That's all I wanted to know, and
the deal is on. But I'll need an advance for expenses. A
thousand ought to do it."

Olliver frowned. "You won't need that much, Crag.
You're going to be living here, as my employee, for the
week before we take off. I have an extra car you can use
for your few trips to the Port. What do you need money
for?"

"A wardrobe, for one thing. A binge, for another."

"I recovered the suitcases you had when you were arrested. They're in your room. As is, you've got a better
wardrobe than you should have, to be looking for a
guard's job. As for the binge, that's out, Crag. You'll
have to stay sober until you've seen this through."

"*Have* to? I don't take orders, Olliver. I have been in
jail, haven't had a drink in a month. Once we get to

Mars I won't take a drink till the job's done, however long it takes. But in between, I'm going to get drunk once, whether you like it or not. If you won't advance me the money, I can get it."

"What if you get in trouble?"

"I'm a solitary drinker. I'll lock myself in my room and you can lock it from the outside, if you're worried."

"A lock that you couldn't get through?"

"A lock I'll have no inclination to get through. You can even put a guard outside the door."

Olliver laughed. "And how explain it to the guard, when he thinks you've been psyched? Psyched men do only social drinking. Besides, you could take care of the guard as easily as the lock, and I haven't any guards to spare. But all right, I'll go along on your having one binge, provided you agree to stay in your room. And that you sober up in time to check yourself out on the J-14."

"Right. Five hundred will be enough, since I've got my clothes back. How about your servants?"

"We have only two inside servants. I'll send them away for a few days. Judeth and I can eat out. But how about your meals? Or will you be eating any?"

"I won't. Where's my room? I'd rather change into some of my own clothes."

"Second floor opposite the head of the stairs. And here's five hundred. The servants will be gone by the time you come back."

Crag took the money and found his room. He checked through his luggage and found that the police had stolen only a few small, if valuable items, nothing that he'd have to replace immediately. He was lucky; a criminal, even if acquitted, was lucky to get any of his belongings back, and he hadn't counted on it.

He changed clothes quickly and went out. The psychological need for a spree was becoming more and more pressing, now that drinks were in sight, and he was in a hurry to get started. He found a shopping district with a liquor store that sold what he wanted. The price was three times what it would have cost him on

Mars and half again what it would have cost in the spacemen's district downtown, but it was still less than two hundred dollars and he paid it without argument.

In his room he drank himself into drugged insensibility and kept himself that way throughout that day and the next by drinking more every time he returned to consciousness. On the morning of the third day he decided he'd had enough and poured what little was left of the liquor down the drain of the sink in his bathroom. There had been no pleasure in the binge, but it had filled a psychic need, and now he could go without drinking until such time as he could do it safely in a more pleasant manner.

He was not quite steady on his feet and his eyes were bloodshot and bleary, but he was under control mentally. He was haunted by a half-memory of having, several times in a half-conscious state, seen Judeth standing beside his bed looking down at him. But he checked the bolt on the door and decided that it must have been hallucination, along with the other dreams and hallucinations he'd had.

In the downstairs hallway he passed Judeth, about to leave. Her look took in his condition and she passed him without speaking. Which was what he wanted.

Olliver wasn't in his study, but Crag wrote a brief note and left it on his desk: "All right, you can get your servants back." He found the kitchen and prepared and ate a sizeable meal, then went back to his room and slept. He woke the next morning feeling fit.

Most of the next few days he spent at the Port inside Olliver's J-14, studying its operation manual and the books on space navigation it contained.

He did his thinking there too, and his planning for the job to come insofar as it could be planned in advance. He also read there books he bought in a book and tape store about Eisen and Menlo.

He already knew, of course, considerable about Eisen. Eisen was a scientist and inventor who, early in his career, must have been struck by the similarities—even the slight similarity of names—between himself and Edison, an inventor of several centuries before, and for that reason had named his workshop Menlo after Edison's Menlo Park. Like Edison, Eisen was an empiric rather than a theoretical scientist; his quick mind saw practical possibilities in what to others were abstract facts and purely mathematical equations. Like Edison, he made things *work* and he himself was an indefatigable worker. But he had gone far beyond Edison in the number and scope of his inventions and had become incomparably richer, one of the richest men in the system. He could have bought and sold governments, but had no interest in politics. Nor in power or glory, solely in his work.

Menlo had grown into a rambling building combining sleeping quarters and workshops, isolated—the nearest Martian village was several miles away and very small —and surrounded by reputedly impregnable defenses. Eisen lived there with an all-male ménage of employees and guards, about thirty of each.

Olliver had been right, Crag knew, in saying that the only way to steal anything from Menlo would be to get employment there first. Even so, there'd be traps within traps, and it was going to be the hardest thing Crag had ever tried. But then, a million dollars was the biggest prize he'd ever tried for.

Meanwhile, Crag kept to himself and avoided contact with the Ollivers, especially Judeth, as much as possible. He paid the servants extra to bring breakfasts to his room on a tray, and his other meals he ate downtown or at the Port restaurant.

After a week he knocked on the door of Olliver's den and was bidden to enter. He asked Olliver if he'd decided on a departure time and Olliver nodded. "Day after tomorrow. Everything in order on the cruiser?"

"Yes," Crag said. "Ready to take off any minute. Want me to arrange clearance?"

"Yes. Make it for 10 A.M. Or as soon after as possible if anything else is clearing then. Need any more money?"

Crag shook his head. "I've got enough to last me till I get to Menlo. If I get the job there I'll be searched—

Eisen's guards are thorough—and don't want to have much on me."

"Right. And they'll investigate whatever you tell them, Crag. Not back of your psycher certificate, although they'll verify that, but your subsequent actions. Have you got a good story as to why you're going to quit your pilot's job when we reach Mars, to take a job that'll pay a lot less?"

"Yes. Meant to check with you on it so your story will back mine if they investigate. Psyched men sometimes lose their space guts, and that's what will have happened to me. I'll have been scared stiff all the way to Mars and never want to go into space again, at any price."

"Good. I'll back you on that, and so will Judeth."

Crag frowned. "Is she going?"

"Yes. Don't worry, there's plenty of room. That's a four-man cruiser. You don't mind?"

"No, if she lets me alone. You may as well tell me now what the object is that you want from Menlo. Why not now? I'm as committed now as I'll ever be. I'm not going to back out no matter what you tell me it is."

"All right. It's a device that looks like a flat pocket flashlight. Blued steel case. Lens in the center of one end—but you can tell it from an ordinary flashlight because the lens is green and is opaque—opaque to light, that is. I could give you a more exact description, but not exact enough for you to fabricate a duplicate in advance."

"And I couldn't take it in with me if I did. Where is it?"

"In the vault off Eisen's private workshop. I don't know just where in the vault but there's a card index to the drawers in the vault and the index is on Eisen's desk. The object is filed under the code designation DIS-1."

"That's all you can give me?"

"Yes. But a few other instructions. Don't steal anything else. Maybe there are other valuable things but I don't want them, and we don't want Eisen to know anything was stolen. And if you get it—"

"*After* I get it."

"All right, after you get it, don't try monkeying with it or using it. Promise me that."

"It'll be easier for me to promise that if I know what it is. My curiosity might get the better of me."

"All right, it's a disintegrator. It's designed to negate the binding force—well, I'm not up on atomic theory so I can't give it to you technically. But it collapses matter into neutronium."

Crag whistled softly. "A disintegrator—and you say Eisen considers it worthless?"

"Yes, because its range is short. The size needed increases with the cube of the distance. The model you're after works up to a distance of only two feet. To make one that would work at twenty feet the apparatus would have to be as big as a house, and to make one that would work at a thousand feet—well, there aren't enough raw materials in the system to make one; it would have to be the size of a small planet.

"Besides, there's a time lag. The ray from the disintegrator sets up a chain reaction in any reasonably homogeneous object it's aimed at, within its range, but it takes seconds for it to get started. No, it's valueless as a weapon, Crag. Take my word for it."

Crag said, "Then the value—if it's worth a million to you—must be in the by-product, neutronium. But what can it be used for?" Crag was familiar with the concept of neutronium, of course; every spaceman was. Even school children knew that some of the stars were made of almost completely collapsed matter weighing dozens of tons to the cubic inch. There were dwarf stars smaller than Earth and weighing more than its sun. But no such collapsed matter existed in the Solar System. Pure neutronium, *completely* collapsed matter, would be unbelievably heavy, heavier than the center of any known star. Certainly, if it could be *handled*, it would have more important uses than weighting chessmen. But when the atoms of an object collapsed wouldn't they simply fall through the interstices of the atoms of whatever you tried to keep it in and simply fall through to the center of the Earth—or of whatever other planet you were on?

Olliver was smiling. "That's not your department to worry about, Crag. I may tell you later, if it fits into my plans. I've given you everything I can that can possibly be helpful to you."

Crag nodded. But he kept on wondering what Olliver's angle was. What value could there be in a weapon that would work only at shorter range than his own left hand, and much less suddenly? Or was there a way of saving and using the neutronium? Well, he'd worry about the answer to those questions when he had the thing in his hands—but before he turned it over to Olliver, even for a million.

The trip to Mars was dull and boring, as are all space trips. Fortunately, the J-14 is relatively a luxury ship and he had a cabin of his own. He spent most of his time in it, except when he was at the controls. He slept as much as he could and spent the rest of his time reading and listening to tapes. He talked as little as possible to Olliver and not at all—except occasionally to answer a direct question—to Olliver's wife.

Crag took the controls for the landing and set the ship down perfectly. He turned to Olliver. "Where'll I get in touch with you?"

"We have reservations at the Phobos. But you're coming that far with us, Crag. I took a room for you too."

"Why? I might as well head right for Menlo."

"Because I've got connections through which I can get you dope on the current situation there. Give me this evening and you can take off tomorrow morning knowing more than you know now."

Crag nodded. At the Phobos Hotel, he went right to his room and stayed there. In the morning he was dressed and ready when his phone rang and Olliver said he was ready.

Olliver met him alone in the main room of the big suite he'd taken for himself and Judeth. He said, "The news is good. Crag. Eisen's on Earth, in the middle of a month's holiday. You'll have two weeks before he gets back. Maybe it'll be easier for you with the cat away."

"Who does the hiring while Eisen's gone?"

"Nobody hires technicians, but the head guard, man named Knutson, is authorized to hire guards. Wasn't able to find out how they're staffed at the moment but the chances are good; they're usually one or two guards under their quota."

Crag said, "I'd rather run into Knutson in the town. Can you tell me how I'll know him if I do?"

"Yes, I met him myself when I visited Menlo six months ago. He's a big man with red hair, diagonal scar on one cheek—forget which. Surly, struck me as being a bully. Need any more money, Crag?"

"I could use a couple of hundred. I've got enough to get there all right, but I might not be able to get a job right away."

Olliver counted out two hundred dollars for him.

Judeth, in a robe, came in as he was putting it into his wallet, about to leave. She put out her hand to him. "Good-by, Crag. Good luck."

Crag wondered why her hand seemed to burn his as he took it. He got out quickly.

The little town of Pranger, population twelve hundred, which was Menlo's only link with civilization (except that, in a sense, Menlo *was* civilization) was in a high valley in the Syrtis Mountains. There were no direct flights between it and Mars City, so Crag had to make his journey in stages and didn't get there until early afternoon. He registered at the inn and had lunch there, then wandered out to see the town.

Not that there was much town to see. Besides two rough-looking taverns and a few stores, it was all miners' cabins. It was a molybdenum mining town and everyone living in it, except those who ran the stores and taverns, worked at the nearby mine. A poor, squalid town. If it was the only place accessible to workers and guards at Menlo, it was no wonder that few cared to work there. But still he didn't want to go directly to the place and apply for a job; that way all his chances would be killed if he were turned down. He'd have no logical excuse to hang around and try again. It would be far better to meet Knutson accidentally and to lay himself open to an offer of a job without having to ask for one. Then his chances wouldn't be ended by a refusal, for he couldn't be refused something he hadn't asked for.

It was early evening when he saw a tall red-haired man passing the inn, and hurried out to follow. He hadn't been able to make out the scar at that distance but the man he was following was better dressed than the miners and he felt sure it would turn out to be Knutson. And when he followed the man into one of the two taverns and was able to see the scar, he knew he was right. And he knew, too, that the big redhead was even more of a bully than Oliver had taken him for, and that meant there was an easy way to make friends with him. If letting oneself get beaten up is easy.

Crag stepped in beside Knutson at the bar and managed to slip and fall against Knutson, spilling part of the drink the man was already holding. But Crag apologized quickly; he had to be careful because he would later have to reveal his psycher certificate to Knutson and meanwhile must do nothing that would make that certificate suspect. A recently psyched man can defend himself if attacked, or, if he is a guard, can attack others in line of duty, but he is not naturally aggressive or on the prod.

But a moment later, again seemingly inadvertently, he again jostled Knutson and made him spill more of the drink. And this time Crag didn't have to apologize because there was no time for it. He managed to ride with the punch in his face so as to let it carry him back away from the bar, but kept from falling. He caught his balance and came in swinging. But with his right hand; he only feinted with his left. He made it look like a good fight, although he could have ended it with a single blow, even of his right hand, almost any time he wanted to. But he made it a good fight and a long fight and let himself be defeated only slowly and far from ignominiously. But finally he was down.

And Knutson, grinning a bloody grin, was helping him

up and saying, "Man, you put up a good scrap, for a guy your size. Damn near beat me. Let me buy you a drink."

So he grinned back and let Knutson lead him to a table and order drinks for both of them. And a few minutes later, after he'd answered Knutson's question as to what he was doing in Pranger, Knutson said, "Man, you don't want to work in a moly mine, a guy that can fight like you can. How'd you like to work at Menlo?"

And, it turned out, Crag would very much like to work at Menlo, for his new-found friend. Checking antecedents, Knutson whooped when Crag showed him the psycher certificate. "Man, that's really good. Only two weeks old. We can skip investigating anything about you before that and you can't have got in much trouble in two weeks. What you been doing?"

Crag explained that, and the head guard said he'd phone Olliver at the Phobos in Mars City early the next morning for a reference. And then, if Crag's prints matched those on the psycher certificate, he was in and could start work as soon as he wanted to. "Don't pay any more than a mine job," Knutson told him, "but it's clean, easy work. Mostly loafing, in fact, as long as you stay awake and alert while you loaf. You on?"

Crag was on.

CHAPTER FIVE

HE COULD have got on simply by going and applying for the job, of course, but it was far better the way he'd done it; he was a friend of Knutson's. The quickest way to make friends with a bully is to get into a fight with him and let him beat you, but after such a tough fight and by so narrow a margin that he respects you. Beat him and he'll hate you; go down easily and he'll be contemptuous of you. And as a friend of Knutson's, Crag got the shift he wanted to start with, the roving night shift that patrolled the interior of Menlo, not the periphery. He got to know every room of the place, except Eisen's private office and laboratory, kept closed and locked while he was away. More than locked, he decided; it must have been well booby-trapped as well. Not even Knutson or Cambridge, the head technician and the man closest to Eisen, knew how to enter it. No one but Eisen ever did enter it, except at his invitation when he was present.

Crag spent three nights and days doing nothing but learning the ropes, the position of every guard at every time, the obvious checks and safeguards, the routine, the layout. A lucky find solved one major future problem for him in advance; on the third floor was a small museum of primitive weapons from Earth. One of them —he'd decide which when the time came—would be just what he needed when the time came for him to get the disintegrator out of Menlo.

The next evening at dinner in the dining room, Knutson asked Crag, "Like fights? Boxing, I mean."

"Sure," Crag said.

"Damn good one on tonight from Mars City, welters. Want to come to my room and watch it on tele?"

"Sure," Crag said.

"It's on at seven. Drop up to my room then and we'll

watch it. If you get there before I do, make yourself at home."

Crag made a careful point of getting there early and making himself at home. He loosened a vacuum tube in the tele-set. When Knutson came in a few minutes later and turned it on, nothing happened. Knutson fiddled with the dials and swore.

Crag said, "I'm pretty good at fixing one of those things. Nobody's working in the main lab now; let's run down there and I'll see if I can get this thing going."

In the lab, he got it out of the case and started fooling with it. But by a few minutes after seven Knutson got restless. "We're missing the fight, Crag. Let's go to the main lounge and catch it on the big set. You can fix that later."

"You go ahead, Knut. I'm so close to getting this fixed I'd really rather stay with it. I'll probably join you there before the fight's over."

He did join Knutson before the fight was over and he had Knutson's teleset working. Also he had several small items in his pockets; a tiny atomic flashlight and a circuit detector, both jury rigged but small and efficient, and a few other things that might be needful.

The next night he settled for going over the outer door of Eisen's office with the flash and the circuit detector and working out the circuits of three separate alarms— or death-traps; it didn't matter which—and that was all he did. He didn't enter the room; he wanted a full night ahead of him for doing that, a night when he didn't have to punch check buttons at various places in the buildings at various times. The next day he talked Knutson into putting him on a day shift.

And the night after that, as early as was safe, he canceled out the three circuits in the door and let himself into Eisen's office, with five hours ahead of him. He spent the first of those hours very carefully going over the office and the laboratory behind it for further alarms or traps. He found and disconnected three. Then he turned his attention to the blank durasteel door of the vault.

It was right beside Eisen's desk and an article lying on the latter gave him a hunch that saved him a lot of time and experimenting. It was a little horseshoe magnet, a toy, that was apparently used as a paperweight. But what if it was more than that? Why couldn't it be the key to a magnetic lock?

He examined the surface of the vault's door inch by careful inch. It being durasteel there were no accidental scratches on it to confuse him. There was only an almost imperceptible flyspeck about a foot to the right of the center door. But flyspecks scrape off and this mark didn't —and besides, there are no flies on Mars. He tried the magnet in various positions about the speck and when he tried holding it with both poles pointing upward and the speck exactly between them the door swung open. Inside were hundreds of drawers of various sizes, each numbered.

Crag turned back to Eisen's desk and in the little card file on a corner of it looked under the code designation Olliver had given him and found the drawer number. A moment later the disintegrator was in his hand. There was no mistaking it, from Olliver's description. It looked for all the world like a tiny pocket flashlight, even smaller than the standard atomic one Crag had stolen from the main laboratory. Except for the lens, which was emerald green and was not transparent. Crag closed the drawer and started to close the vault door and then stopped. He had time to fabricate a dummy duplicate and he might as well follow Olliver's suggestion that he leave a substitute. True, if Eisen ever tried to use the device he'd discover the substitution, but if he made periodic checkups just to make sure that nothing was missing, he'd simply look at the duplicate and not check its workings. And the longer before he might discover the theft, the better.

He carried the thing into the private laboratory and went to work there. Eisen couldn't possibly have provided better equipment for a burglar who wanted to leave a duplicate of whatever small object he stole. Given time, Crag could probably have taken the thing apart and made an actual working duplicate. But he settled for a really good outward duplicate and when he had finished it, he made sure there was not even the slightest sign left that he had used the workbench or moved a single tool. He placed the duplicate in the drawer and closed the vault, reconnected the alarms or traps except those at the door, and then waited quietly in darkness until he heard the guard pass on a round. Ten minutes later, the door again a deathtrap, he was safely back in his room. In office and workshop, there was no trace of his having visited there—unless Eisen tried to work the disintegrator or had a careful inventory of all the scrap metal in the workshop's junk bins. The several other things he had to do could wait till tomorrow, and he got two hours of sleep.

Getting the disintegrator safely out of the place was the most important thing the next day, and the easiest. The third-floor primitive weapons museum room was on his rounds. He picked the stoutest bow, a relatively modern twentieth century hunting bow, and a heavy hunting arrow. He taped the little disintegrator on the arrow just behind the steel head. Shot through the window it carried far over the electrified fence and down into a gully out of sight from any point in Menlo. Unless it had broken in the arrow's landing—and he had wrapped it in cloth against that contingency—the disintegrator was now safe for him to recover at leisure. A quick stop in the main workshop while the technicians were at lunch enabled him to replace the atomic flashlight and to throw in the scrap bins the parts of the circuit detector, which he had already disassembled, and to get rid of the few other small things he had taken.

But he didn't want to arouse suspicion by quitting suddenly. Or, worse, getting himself fired, which he could do only by conduct that would be suspiciously out of character for a psyched man. He took the safe way. The following morning he reported himself as having a severe headache and feeling dizzy. Knutson took him to the dispensary and left him there to find the technician who ran it and who had a lay knowledge of medicine. Crag took advantage of the temporary solitude by making free use of two drugs, one of them belladonna and the other a quick-acting cathartic, he found in the supply cabinet.

"Looks like rill fever," said the technician, examining Crag's contracting pupils. "Ever had it before?"

Crag grinned wryly. "I wouldn't remember. It might be on my record."

The technician looked at Knutson. "If it is, he'll have diarrhea starting within a few hours. And if it is, he'd better get to Mars City for treatment. I can't take care of him here, or even make a biopsy to make sure that's what it is."

"Maybe we shouldn't wait," Knutson said. "I can run him into Mars City and make sure."

"He's better off if he doesn't travel till this first attack is over. If that's what it is, he'll be all right by tomorrow and it's always several days at least before there's a second attack. As long as he gets a checkup—and treatment if that's what it is—before a second attack, he'll be all right."

Crag got worse and the expected diarrhea lasted most of the afternoon, but in the morning he felt better, much better. Knutson got his pay for him and even offered to forego searching Crag and his luggage to save time, but Crag insisted on the search, saying he didn't want to be suspected in case, at a later date, anything at Menlo turned out to be missing. He also turned down Knutson's offer of a lift into Pranger by heli insisting that the walk would make him feel better. Well out of sight of Menlo, he hid his suitcases along the path and circled around to the gulley where the arrow had landed and recovered it. He pocketed the disintegrator and buried the arrow in the sand.

He didn't try out the disintegrator so near Menlo for Olliver had not happened to mention whether or not its operation was silent; quite possibly it wasn't. He waited until he was back near his luggage and then took it from his pocket, aimed it at a bush half a dozen feet away and pushed the thumb slide. Nothing happened until, gradually, he moved it nearer to the bush. When he was within a few inches of two feet away the outlines of the bush became misty and then it was no longer there, nor was there any trace of the bush left on the sand from which it had grown. Olliver had not lied about the nature of the device nor about the limitation of its range. It might be of value to a criminal in disposing of a dead body, but almost any other weapon, even a knife, was more efficient in killing. It didn't look worth a million dollars to Crag, but that was Olliver's business.

That afternoon in Mars City he made his first business following through on his alibi for quitting the job, just in case. He went to a clinic and waited while a biopsy was made and checked. He was told he did not have rill fever and that the symptoms must have been something else. He promised to return for a full-scale checkup if the symptoms returned.

And he called Knutson to give him the news, as he'd promised. If he didn't Knutson might wonder, and anyway there was no use closing that door. He didn't have the million yet and if he got it, it might not last forever. It would be handy to be able to go back to Menlo and work there again any time he might want to. Knutson tried to talk him into coming back then, but Crag said that even though it wasn't rill fever he'd had, it had been something and he'd rather, for a while, work in Mars City so he'd be near a clinic if there was a recurrence.

He called Olliver's hotel and got him on the phone. "Crag speaking," he said. "I've got it."

"Wonderful, Crag! Can you come right around?"

"Have you got your end of it, there in the room?"

"Here? Of course not. It'll take me until tomorrow afternoon to—"

"I'll phone you tomorrow afternoon."

"Wait, Crag. Where are you—?"

Crag hung up.

It was late the following afternoon when he called. Olliver said, "Crag, don't hang up! Listen to me. That much money in cash is hard to raise. Most of my investments are on Earth, and I'm trying—"

"How much have you got, there in the hotel?"

"Half. And it'll take me at least a few days more to raise the rest."

"All right," Crag said. "If you've got half I'll trust you for the rest. Is anyone else there now?"

"Just Judeth. Can you come right away?"

Crag said that he would, and got there in five minutes. Oliver, his face tense with eagerness, let him in. "You brought it?"

Crag nodded and looked around. Judeth, dressed even more revealingly than she had been the first time he had seen her at Olliver's house in Albuquerque on Earth, lounged on a brocaded sofa staring at him with an unreadable expression.

Olliver turned to her. "We'll take his word that he has it. Get him the money, dear."

Judeth went into an adjoining room of the suite and came back with an inch-thick sheaf of money. She held it out to Crag. "Five hundred thousand, all there. Count it."

Crag thrust it into a pocket. "If I'm trusting you for the second half of the million I might as well take your count on the first half. All right. Olliver, here's your toy."

Olliver's hand trembled slightly as he took it. "Good boy, Crag. And you don't think they'll miss anything from Menlo?"

"They'll never miss it, unless Eisen tries actually to use the duplicate I left in place of that one. Now about that second half million. When and where do I collect?"

Olliver said, "Sit down, Crag," and went over to sit on the sofa beside his wife. "Let me explain part of my plans, and make a suggestion. First, I can get you the rest of the money within twenty-four hours of the time we get back to Earth. I've got it there; it's just a matter of turning investments into cash."

"All right," Crag said. "And when do you plan to get back to Earth?"

"Leaving tomorrow. But with one other place to go before we go to Earth. Whole trip will take a us a week. But there's the second part of the suggestion. Why not come with us?"

"What's your other stop?"

"The asteroid belt. Just the near edge of it. I want to land on one small asteroid."

"To test the disintegrator?"

Crag nodded slowly, wondering why he hadn't thought of so simple an answer to getting neutronium in handleable form. Disintegrate an entire tiny asteroid and its atoms would collapse inward on themselves, since the asteroid would be in no gravitational field except its own; it would collapse into a tiny ball that could be carried back in a spaceship—providing it was a small enough ball that its mass, which would become weight again when you brought it back with you to a planet, wasn't great enough to crash the ship in landing it. Simple, once you thought of it. How come Eisen hadn't? Or maybe Eisen had, but hadn't seen any value in or use for neutronium. Olliver had something up his sleeve there too.

"All right," Crag said. "What time tomorrow do you clear?"

"Does noon suit you?"

"Any time," Crag said. "I'll meet you at the ship. You haven't used it? It's still in the same berth?"

"Yes, and refueled and ready. Glad you're coming, Crag. I've got something really important to talk to you about, and that will give us plenty of chance. We'll see you at the ship then."

Crag still had time to go to two different banks and, at each, to stash a sizeable fraction of the half million. And then he spent a quiet and thoughtful evening wondering, among other things, why he'd bothered to do so. He didn't trust Olliver—for the simple reason that he didn't trust anyone—and it was quite possible Olliver might be inviting him on that trip with the idea of recovering one half million dollars and saving another. But if Olliver did succeed in killing him, what difference could it make to Crag whether the money was on his person or safe back in Mars City? Well, it might make a difference at that, if he let Olliver know that he'd stashed the bulk of the money. Yes, he'd take that precaution and every other one he could think of. But he'd still have to sleep and. . . . He shrugged; when you shoot for big money you take big chances and you might as well not worry about them. Possibly Olliver would be afraid to try to kill him, knowing that if he failed he himself wouldn't have long to live. And possibly Olliver's plan in connection with the disintegrator really was one that made peanuts out of a million dollars.

He slept well.

He was checking over the J-14 when Olliver and Judeth arrived the next day. Judeth immediately went to her cabin to change from street clothes into coveralls for the trip. Olliver sank into the co-pilot seat next to Crag, and leaned back. "Lots of time yet. And course is plotted."

"Where?"

"Simply the nearest point in the asteroid belt. When we get there we simply look till we find one the right size."

Crag said, "One weighing less than half a ton. That is, if you intend to bring it back. That's about all the extra payload this ship can make a safe Earth-landing with. Or do you intend to jettison anything already aboard?"

Olliver smiled. "I'm not planning to jettison anything aboard. But I'm surprised, Crag—and pleased—that you had the nerve and judgment to come along. A lesser man might figure I might leave him out there, if I got the chance, to save myself a half million."

Crag grunted. "I'll take my chances."

"You won't be taking any. Crag, this thing is *big*, and if you want to ride with me on it, you can be big too. That lousy million won't mean a thing to you. You'll have something more important than money. Power."

"And you?"

"I'll have more power. More power than any man has

ever had in the history of mankind. I'll—well, I'm not telling you the details now, Crag. After we've been to the belt, after I'm sure of two certain points. Crag, what do you think of Judeth?"

"What does it matter?"

"I want to know."

Crag said, "I hate all women."

"And perhaps Judeth more than any other?"

"No," Crag lied. "Why?"

Olliver shrugged. "Forget it. Well, since you're in the driver's seat, might as well take off. Cold on the stroke of noon, and here are the coordinates. I'll tell Judeth to strap in."

He headed for the double cabin, and a moment later came back and strapped himself in the co-pilot chair. "She's strapping down in there," he said. And then thoughtfully, "A beautiful woman, Crag, but also a brilliant one. Never trust brilliant women; that's something I'm learning. Well, Crag, what do you think about my proposition?"

"I'll wait till I hear it. All right, five seconds of twelve. Four. Three. Two. . . . "

Crag found the trip dull. So apparently did Judeth; she spent most of the time in her cabin. Only Olliver seemed eager, operating under a barely suppressed excitement that made him so restless that he seemed unable to sit still or to concentrate. At times he seemed lost in a dream from which he had to shake himself with difficulty if asked a question.

Such as when they were nearing the belt. Craig, at the controls, was decelerating and, at the same time, turning to match speed and directions with the asteroids revolving in it. Some were already showing in the detectors. "How big a one shall I pick?" he asked.

"Huh? Oh. It doesn't matter much. Few hundred tons. Size of a house, maybe."

"We can't take it back with us, no matter how small it gets, if you pick one with that much mass."

"We're not going to. Just a test."

"Then why not pick a big one? I can find Ceres for you.

Little under five hundred miles in diameter."

"Take too long, Crag. This isn't an instantaneous chain reaction; there's a time lag, remember. If my information is correct, it'll take at least an hour for one of a few hundred tons."

Crag remembered that it had taken several seconds for the bush he'd tried it on; it seemed reasonable. He'd never told Olliver that he himself had disobeyed instructions and had already tested it.

There were asteroids all around them now, showing in the detectors at distances as close as a mile or two. Crag studied them and picked out one approximately the size Olliver had asked for, began the delicate maneuvering that would put the ship alongside it, exactly matching its speed and direction.

Olliver watched breathlessly. "You've got it, Crag."

Crag nodded and shut off the power. The spaceship and the asteroid, held close together by the few pounds of gravitational pull between the masses, would continue through space side by side until power was again applied to the ship.

Olliver clapped him on the shoulder. "Nice work, Crag. All right, let's get our suits on. I'll tell Judeth."

There would have been no real need for all of them to have left the ship for the test, but in any case they all had to put on space suits. A ship as small as a J-14 has no airlock; it is more economical, on the few occasions, which one leaves it in space or on an airless body, simply to exhaust the air from the entire ship and let the air-maker rebuild an atmosphere after one's return—and before removing the space suit.

Crag was adjusting the transparent helmet of his suit when Judeth came out of the cabin, already suited. Olliver asked, "We all ready? I'll start letting the air out." They heard his voice now, of course, in their helmet radios. "You're both coming out, aren't you?"

Judeth said, "I wouldn't miss it for a million." And Crag nodded.

Olliver stood watching the pressure indicator and in a minute or two he said, "All right," and pushed the lever

that activated the door mechanism. Standing in the doorway he adjusted the grapples on his space boots to enable him to stand on the asteroid and jumped lightly
across to it, abruptly, once outside the artificial gravity
field of the ship, seeming grotesquely to be standing at
right angles to the floor of the ship.

Unspacewise, he had not carried the mooring line and
grapple, and the backlash of his jump sent the spaceship
drifting away from the asteroid; had he been alone he
would have had to jump back quickly before it drifted
out of jumping distance. Crag called out to him and
threw him the grapple and, when Olliver had attached
it, reeled in until the ship was again only a few feet
away from the surface of the asteroid, and safely an-
chored. He jumped down then, and Judeth followed
him.

Olliver was walking rapidly toward the opposite side
of the asteroid. Before following, Crag looked about him.
Time and its relation to distance were strange in so tiny
a world as this. A walk of thirty yards could carry you
from night to day and back to night again. The ship was
moored at the sunset line; Olliver had stopped at the opposite sunrise line and called out, "Here we go," and
Crag knew he was holding the distintegrator down to
the surface of the asteroid and flicking the switch.

Would it really, Crag wondered, disintegrate an object the size of this as easily as, even if more slowly than,
the bush he'd tried it on on Mars? Why not, if what it
started was a chain reaction that would go through any
reasonably homogeneous substance? It had disintegrated
all of the bush, although áll of it had not been within
two feet of the disintegrator. Good God, Crag thought,
what if he had held the disintegrator closer to the ground,
within two feet of it! Would it have started a chain reaction that would, however long it took to do it, destroyed
the Planet Mars? Why not, if it was going to work on an
asteroid like this? The difference was only a matter of
size and size doesn't matter in a chain reaction. A chill
went down his spine at the thought of the risk he had
unwittingly taken—the risk of not only having destroyed

himself but a whole planet and having caused the death of almost fifty million people.

Olliver was coming back now and Judeth moved to meet him, so Crag followed. They stopped in the middle of the day side. Olliver was bending down again and Crag looked to see if he was going to apply the disintegrator to another point. But Olliver was merely laying a six-inch pocket rule against the surface of the asteroid and, with a piece of chalk was making marks opposite both ends of the rule. "So we can tell quicker when it starts to happen—if it does. If those chalk marks get less than six inches apart, then it's happening."

"And then what?" Crag asked. "We'd better run for the ship before the asteroid goes out from under us?"

"Yes, but there'll be no hurry; we'll have at least half an hour."

"And then what?" Crag asked again.

"And then—Wait, I *think* those marks are closer together, but wait till we're absolutely sure, and then I'll tell. Look—" He grabbed Judeth's space-suited arm. "Look, my dear, *aren't* they closer? Isn't it shrinking?"

"I—I think it is. And isn't the horizon closer?"

Olliver straightened and looked toward the horizon and Judeth's face turned toward Crag, her eyes staring strangely at him. He got the idea she wanted to ask him a question but didn't dare—and was trying to find the answer by staring into his eyes. He met her gaze squarely, defiantly, but it puzzled him.

Olliver said, "I think— Well, why think? Another minute at the outside and we'll be sure."

And then, his voice very calm, he said, "Yes, those marks are almost half an inch closer together. It works." He stepped back away from them and his eyes went to Crag. He said, "Crag, that million of yours is wastepaper now. But how would you like to be my hatchet man, second in command of the Solar System?"

Crag looked at him without answering, wondering if Olliver could be mad. The thought must have showed in his face, for Olliver shook his head. "I'm not crazy, Crag. Nor do I know any important commercial use for neutronium—that was camouflage. But Crag—think of this—

"Just one of these little gadgets set up in a hidden place on each of the occupied planets, each with a separate radio control so it can be triggered off from wherever I may be. That's all it will take. If it works on an asteroid —and it does—it'll work on an object of any size. A chain reaction doesn't differentiate between a peanut and a planet."

Crag stared, wondering how he had been so stupid not to have guessed.

Olliver said, "You might as well know all of it, Crag. There isn't any political party behind me. That was just talk. But from now on, once I get this set up, there aren't going to *be* any political parties. There'll just be—me. But I'll need help, of course, and you're the man I'd rather have for my *segundo,* in spite of—"

Suddenly he laughed and his voice changed. "Judeth, my dear, that's useless."

Crag looked quickly toward Judeth and saw that she'd pulled a heatgun from the pocket of her space suit and was pointing it at Olliver.

Olliver chuckled. "I thought it was about time for you to show your true colors, my dear. And I thought this might be the time for it. I found that little toy in your space suit some hours ago and I took the charge out of it. Go ahead and pull the trigger. Or are you pulling it already?"

She was pulling it; standing alongside of her Crag could see that the trigger was all the way back against the guard, and the muzzle was aimed right at Olliver. Crag saw too that her face was pale—but he thought it was pale from anger rather than from fear.

She said to Olliver, "All right, you beat me on that one. But someone will stop you, somehow. Don't you realize that you can't do what you plan without destroying at least one planet to show them you're not bluffing? Millions of lives—billions, if Earth has to be one of the planets you destroy! If you destroy Earth, you'll kill off three-fourths of the human race, just to rule the ones that are left. You must be mad."

Olliver laughed. There was a heatgun in his own hand now, held not too carelessly, so it covered both of them as he took a step backward.

"She's a spy, Crag. A spy for the Guilds. I've known it all along—and kept her on a string. She married me because they wanted her to watch me. Well—I let her, and let her help me, and now God help her. Take that gun away from her, Crag."

The gun was empty and the command meaningless; Crag knew Olliver was testing him. Olliver was making him line up, one way or the other.

Crag hesitated; was Olliver mad, or would he really run the system and would he really make Crag his second in command? And did Crag *want* that, at the price of destroying one or more worlds? Killing men was one thing; he'd killed plenty of them. But destroying worlds, killing entire populations—

Olliver said, "Your last chance, Crag, or I'll burn both of you instead of just Judeth. Don't think I've been blind to the fact that you two are crazy about each other, and have been pretending to hate one another so I wouldn't guess. Well, you can have her, Crag, but she'll be dead when you get her. Or would you rather have power worth more than billions?" He laughed. "And any woman, *all* the women, you want."

Definitely the asteroid was shrinking in size. Olliver was standing closer to them, though he had not moved. He said, "Well, Crag?" and stepped back to reach a safe distance again.

If the attached glove of Crag's space suit had not prevented, he could have thrown his metal hand and had at least an even chance of its striking before Olliver could trigger the heatgun. As it was, there was only one other chance, and whether they both survived it depended on whether the woman's reflexes would be as fast or almost as fast, as Crag's own. He turned to her and reached out with his right hand, as though for the gun she still held, but instead his hand flashed up to her shoulder and he pushed hard and snapped "Night side!"

The push carried her off balance and two steps backward; only another step was needed to carry her below the dwindling horizon and out of range of Olliver's weapon. Crag himself took a diagonally different course. And, as he'd hoped, the heat beam lanced out between them, hitting neither. A fraction of a second later both were in darkness on the side of the asteroid away from the sun. Safe, for the moment.

In his helmet radio, Crag heard Olliver curse. And then laugh. Olliver said contemptuously, "You're a damned fool, Crag. Turning down an offer like I made you—for a woman and a chance to be a hero, for a few minutes." He laughed again and this time there seemed to be genuine amusement in his laughter. "It's a small world, Crag, and getting smaller. How long do you think it will be big enough to hide behind?"

There was no point in answering, and Crag didn't. He stood still for the moment letting his eyes get acustomed to the almost perfect darkness, a darkness ameliorated only by faint starlight and light reflected dimly from a few other small but distant asteroids in orbits paralleling their own. One, he noticed, quite small in apparent size because of either genuine smallness or distance, seemed to be coming closer, growing larger. His eyes dropped and swept about the lessening horizon as he turned. No sign of Olliver; there wouldn't be. Olliver would take no chances in coming around to the night side where, because for at least a moment he'd be completely blind, his weapon would be of no advantage to him.

He could, of course, simply go back to the spaceship and maroon them here, but Crag didn't think Olliver would. Olliver would want the satisfaction of killing them in person; he felt sure of that. And it would be safe and easy for him to get them when the asteroid had shrunk enough. You can't hide behind an object the size of a basketball.

But where was Judeth? He looked around again. Had she gone toward the spaceship in the hope that she might round the opposite side of the asteroid and get a chance to board it?

Crag turned to look that way, and swore. The sunward side of the spaceship glinted—far away. It was moving outward from the asteroid, getting smaller in the distance. Not under power; it was drifting, but drifting fast. Had he misjudged Olliver, after all? Was Olliver simply going away and leaving them to die as soon as the air supply of their suits was exhausted?

A sudden bellow of rage in his helmet radio answered the question for him. Olliver was still on the other side, the day side, of the asteroid and he had just seen the dwindling ship.

And at that moment a hand closed on Crag's arm, and Judeth's voice said, "Crag, I'm sorry. I *had* to push it off. There wasn't a chance for us to get into it; the hatch was way on his side, the day side, and he'd have—"

"Wait," Crag said.

He groped in the darkness until he found the switch of her helmet radio, turned it off, and then his own. He leaned forward so the front plate of his helmet touched hers and said, "While our helmets touch we can hear one another, and Olliver can't hear us. You *can* hear me?"

"Yes." her voice was flat, but not frightened. "But what does it matter about Olliver? We're all dead, all three of us. I'm sorry, Crag. I had to do it."

"What did you do with the heatgun?"

"My pocket. Here. But it's not loaded."

Crag took it and hefted it. It was a little lighter than the missile he would have preferred, but his spacesuit kept him from using that one. He thought he'd be able to throw the gun fairly straight.

He said, "Wait here," and squeezed Judeth's arm gently, then turned and started back for the day side. The asteroid was shrinking fast now, only about twenty feet in diameter. He had to crouch to keep his head from showing as he neared the borderline between light and darkness. Then, as he stood only a step away from the edge, he abruptly straightened, the gun held back ready to throw.

Olliver stood there, turning in a tight circle, trying to watch all sides at once. The gun left Crag's hand, and didn't miss; Olliver's helmet shattered.

He took a deep breath and walked the rest of the way. He turned on the radio switch of his helmet and called out, "Judeth. Is your radio on? Can you hear me?"

"Yes, Crag." She was coming. She looked down at Olliver's body and shuddered. "He was a mad dog, Crag. And yet—I wasn't sure, clear till the last minute, after we landed here. I suspected him, but I was never sure, until then. I thought maybe he really meant—"

"Was he right about you being a spy for the Guild Party?"

"No. Nor for anyone else. I fell in love with him and married him, three years ago. And I believed in his new party that was going to end corruption and bring back decent government."

"You were still in love with him?"

"No, not for months now. Almost a year. But by the time I'd fallen out of love, I'd begun to suspect him. And stuck with him in case I was right and in case I could stop him. And thank God I did. He'd have destroyed most of the human race just to have absolute rule over whatever was left of it. You consider yourself a criminal, Crag; you're not one at all, compared to him."

She turned to stare up at the dwindling spaceship. "There's no chance of your reaching it and bringing it back?"

"Not now. I could jump after it, but the chance of hitting it would be one in a million." He picked up Olliver's fallen heatgun. "If this was a reactor gun, so I could steer myself in space—but it isn't, and a heat gun doesn't help. Well—"

"Crag, we've got to destroy that disintegrator. There's only a chance in a billion that our bodies will ever be found here, but if they are, that'll be found too and—someone might discover what it is and get the same idea Olliver had."

"All right." Crag reached down and went through pockets of Olliver's space suit, came up with the disintegrator. "Guess this heatgun will melt it to a lump of—Wait, might as well use it first. This small world of ours is getting smaller. No use having it unnecessarily crowded."

He flipped the thumb switch of the disintegrator, held it a foot above Olliver's body, moved it slowly from the shattered helmet to the space-booted feet. "We don't need him for company, do we?"

"Crag, a wonderful idea. Will you use it on me—in a few minutes?"

"A few minutes? The air in these suits should be good for another half hour, Judeth. Why be in a hurry?"

"My air's giving out already, Crag. Olliver must have tampered with it as well as with the charge in the heat-gun I had in my spacesuit pocket. He must have *known* I'd turn against him when he told us his plans. Even if he didn't really think I was a spy."

Her breath was coming hard now. "Crag, you *will* use the disintegrator on me, please? I just don't want to be found ever, looking the way a woman looks when she asphyxiates."

"Sure," Crag said.

"And—I'm afraid, Crag. Will you put your arms around me?"

He did, and he didn't hate her at all.

She clung to him. She was panting now, fighting for every breath. She said, "Good-by, Crag, I won't make you listen to—" She shut off her helmet radio.

Less than a minute later she was limp in his arms. Crag put her down gently and, as she had requested him to do, used the disintegrator. This time he didn't watch.

Then he put the disintegrator down, used Olliver's heatgun on it for a full minute at only a few inches, until it was a shapeless bubbling blob of molten metal.

His little world was almost too small to stand on now, but for another few minutes he managed to stand, looking upward at the bright little stars in the big black sky. He was breathing hard now; the oxygen in his own suit was nearly exhausted now and he didn't have more than another ten minutes or so to live. Judeth must have been wrong in thinking that air had been taken from her supply deliberately; Olliver would have had no reason to short the supply in Crag's. Probably both or even all three suits had been short of oxygen through Olliver's negligence, which wouldn't have mattered had the space-ship remained for them to return to.

The asteroid was less than a yard in diameter now, and Crag gave up trying to stand on it and sat down.

And smaller, until he got off it and looked and laughed at the poor shrinking thing, the world that had been an asteroid as big as Olliver's house when they'd landed on it.

Fought for breath and got ready to die. Alone, but that didn't matter, so long had he lived alone.

Held the small world in his hand now, the size of an orange. Laughed a final time as he put it in the pocket of his space suit, wondering what they'd ever make of finding it there, a three-inch ball with hundreds of tons of mass, if they ever found him here.

Slid into blackness as dark as the sky but unrelieved by stars.

And died.

CHAPTER SIX

ENTERING his several millionth solar system, he had expected nothing unusual. Why should he have? It seemed like any other.

He passed two cold dead giant planets, one with a ring around it. He had seen many such, and knew how they had been formed. He passed the orbit of Jupiter, but Jupiter was on the other side of the sun; otherwise, on certain of Big Jupe's moons, he might have encountered sooner that for which he had long since ceased to search, life other than his own.

Next toward the still distant yellow sun, a belt of asteroids. Chunks of rock like him, but unlike him, only lifeless rock, unthinking, unsentient. Some many times larger than he, some much smaller. In such a belt of orbiting asteroids he himself had been one of thousands until had happened the molecular accident that, billions of years ago, had brought consciousness to him and had made him unlike the others.

This belt had been formed the same way and was no different, he thought at first. Then, suddenly:

From only light-seconds away, at a point along the inner edge of the asteroid belt, he perceived *something*. Something confused and muddled, but which was, which had to be consciousness. Alien consciousness. Another being besides himself. Or beings; there seemed to be several of them.

Quickly he dropped into subspace and almost instantaneously reappeared in normal space a dozen miles from the point from which he had detected these emanations of consciousness. It was an asteroid, a small one. He matched his speed to its and maintained his distance from it, to observe. His reason for not approaching closer was not caution; it was simply that at this convenient distance he could observe as well as from any nearer point; he could perceive, through a sense that was not sight for he had no seeing organs, not only the outward appearance but the very arrangement of the molecules of the asteroid and the things or beings upon it or attached to it.

He was aware that a change was taking place in the molecular arrangement of the asteroid itself, a simple chain reaction that was collapsing not only the molecules but the very atoms of which the molecules were made in upon themselves, a reaction that once started would now continue until the asteroid was reduced to a tiny chunk of collapsed matter a minute fraction of the original size of the original form of the asteroid. This did not hold his interest; he was familiar with such reactions and could himself instigate or reverse them.

Nor did his interest center upon the subject moored to the collapsing asteroid, although in the absence of the alien life forms, it would have interested him considerably in that, by the fact that it was an artificial construction, it would have been his first discovery of evidence that sentient beings other than himself existed anywhere in the universe. But here were the sentient beings themselves and he concentrated his scannings upon them. One of them was at that very moment detaching the mooring line of the artificial construction from the asteroid and giving it an impetus that sent it drifting out into space.

The being in question, and the other two like it, were, he perceived, themselves encased within smaller constructions. Most parts of these smaller constructions, he could tell from their molecular structure, were flexible. As were most parts of the bodies of the beings inside the constructions. Strange, complicated bodies they were. And fragile, so fragile; there was an arrangement to produce heat within the constructions that housed them, and they held a gas; apparently both the gas and heat were necessary to these beings. He analyzed the gas and found it to be mostly oxygen and carbon dioxide; there were traces of other elements. The beings drew this gas into their bodies and exhaled it less much of its oxygen content; a container of concentrated oxygen automatically replaced the oxygen absorbed by the bodies inside the constructions. It seemed a very strange and limiting arrangement. There were planets, many of them, with oxygen atmospheres and with the degree of heat the construction supplied and held in. On such planets these beings could live without the artificial casings that now held them and it came to him that they must be from such a planet—possibly inhabited by others like them—and that their presence here on an airless asteroid in the cold of space was temporary, their casings designed to permit survival in—

Survival? Whence had that concept come to him? Until now, death had been a meaningless concept, one that had never occurred to him, but now suddenly he knew what it meant and knew that these beings he was observing lived for a short time only and then ceased to be. And that he now knew this was only in part a deduction from the study of their physical bodies, so it meant that their thoughts—at first a meaningless jumble of utterly alien concepts—were beginning to be understandable to him.

And then, quite suddenly, there were only two beings, two focuses of consciousness. One of the three had quite suddenly—died. His body had suddenly become a piece of lifeless rather than living matter. Another of the three had propelled an object that had broken a rigid and shatterable part of the first one's protective casing, and this had been the result. Now a device was being used on the dead one and his casing that was setting up the chain reaction of molecular collapse. Apparently these people had only slight mental powers, to use a physical contraption for so simple a matter.

He concentrated his study on the two remaining. One of them seemed to be having—the concept *pain* came to him, although he did not yet understand it fully—and the pain seemed to be connected with the fact that the oxygen content of the gas within its casing was lessening. And since the reserve of oxygen seemed exhausted, this being, too, would soon die, and he concentrated his study upon it while it lasted, which wasn't long.

The remaining one again used the device and again there wasn't even a body left. Were these creatures all so ephemeral?

Now, with only one of them left, the thoughts were more nearly clear. Completely alien concepts, though. With another device, one for producing heat, this last one was destroying the thing that had produced molecular collapse in the bodies of the first two.

Why? Again, he tried to probe the surviving mind, and found the thoughts confusing. They were completely alien concepts, behind which he sensed something fierce and wild. And then something calm and waiting, and again the pain. And nothing. The third being had ceased to be.

It had all happened so incredibly quickly. After these eons to have found three living beings, three sentient entities, and then to have had them all three flicker out as quickly as meteorites entering an atmosphere! For a moment he considered going on, searching for the planet from which these beings, he had already deduced, must have come. But there was something else he could try first.

Carefully and leisurely he examined the structure of the body of the last of the three to die, and the only one of the three which had not been disintegrated. Closely studied, much became obvious. He found two spongy organs that held air and muscles that gave bellows action to draw in the air and push it out again. He synthesized oxygen and teleported it into the casing's oxygen container and then activated the muscles that controlled the spongy organs. The being breathed. Simultaneously he activated an organ of heavy muscle which served as a pump to circulate a stream of fluid throughout the body. After a while he found he could cease to activate those muscles and they continued of themselves.

The top or conscious level of the being's mind remained dormant, passive, but the creature lived. He probed into the lower, the memory level of the mind and found with satisfaction that now, without the conflict of emotion or surface thought, his task was much easier. In Crag's memories he found the answers to his questions about the puzzling series of events upon the asteroid. He learned who the other two beings had been and why the three of them had been there.

He learned everything Crag remembered of Crag's own history and everything Crag had ever read or heard of human and planetary history, even the things Crag's conscious mind had long since forgotten. He got to know Crag, in the process, better than one entity has ever known another.

And, in the process, he found that he was no longer alone.

CHAPTER SEVEN

CRAG awoke as an animal wakes, suddenly and completely aware of himself. But things were wrong—rather, things were right that should have been wrong—and he neither opened his eyes nor moved a muscle. He was breathing air, and he shouldn't have been. He'd been dying for lack of it; he should be dead now instead of awakening.

Besides that, he was lying on hard rock, with enough of a gravitational pull to hold his space suit as firmly against it as though he was on Earth again. Not even the largest asteroid had that strong a gravity; could he be back on Earth? Another spaceship could conceivably have found him and picked him up before he died, the air in his suit could have been replenished, but . . . it didn't make sense. His space suit would have been taken off him long before making planetfall. Or—another possibility occurred to him; he could be lying on a pile of rock in the ore locker of one of the wildcat mining ships that worked the asteroid belt for uranium and—

"No, Crag," said a voice inside his mind. "You are safe, but you are neither on Earth nor on a ship."

Crag opened his eyes and looked up—into space. Into blackness lighted by untwinkling stars and a distant sun. He sat up and looked around him. Again he was on the surface of an asteroid, but this time a much larger one. From what he could see of it from a sitting position, it was possibly up to a mile in diameter—but still far too small to have a gravity field equal to, or anywhere near, the normal Earth-gravity he was feeling.

"The gravity is artificial, Crag," said the voice inside his mind. "About the strength of that of your native planet. Would you prefer a lesser one, like that of the fourth planet, the one you think of as Mars?"

"Who are you?" Crag asked aloud. He wondered for

a brief moment if he was really dead, and if this was some mad, weird dream in an afterlife; then he discarded the idea. This was real, and he was not dead.

"I have no name," said the voice. "I am what you think of as an asteroid on which you are sitting. And, in a sense, I am an asteroid, but from another solar system very far from here. But I am a sentient being, as you are."

"Siliceous life?" Crag asked. "But why did you—?"

"Is life based on silica any stranger than life based on carbon? As to why I saved you—brought you back to life, really—call it curiosity, if nothing more. You are the first alien being I ever encountered."

"Then—you came along and found me after what happened on the—the other asteroid?"

"While it was happening. But it was only confusion to me, until it was all over; I did not know what was going on there. I know everything that happened, though, now, from your thoughts and memories while you slept after I brought you back to life. You're finding it difficult to believe all this, but it is true. And you are not dead nor are you now dreaming." There was a slight pause and then the voice said, "That space suit is hurting you; you've had it on too long. Shall I enclose an atmosphere inside a force field so you can take it off for a while?"

"I'm all right," Crag said. He started to get to his feet, but found himself pinned to the ground by one side of his space suit, the side which had the pocket into which he had put the collapsed smaller asteroid. He grinned and said, "Except that I'm stuck. I've got a few hundred tons in my pocket, in this gravity. Could you unstick me?"

There was no answer but he felt suddenly very light, almost completely weightless. He took the orange-sized sphere of neutronium out of his pocket and put it down. Then as he stood up, his weight returned to Earth-normal.

"Damn clever," Crag said. "Do you do that without machinery?"

"I never heard of machinery, Crag, until I learned about it from your mind and memory while you were asleep. From your mind I learned—"

"Damn you," said Crag viciously. "Get out of my mind."

There was abrupt silence, a sense of withdrawal. And, after a moment, the voice spoke again, but this time Crag heard it as a sound, not thought; a vibratory manipulation of the air inside his helmet. "I am sorry," it said. "I should have realized that you would resent my sharing your thoughts. But without reading your thoughts, when I first returned you to life and while you slept, I could not be communicating with you now. I shall not enter your mind again."

Crag frowned. "Why didn't you leave me dead? What do you want of me?"

"I did not know then; it was only curiosity, the wish to find out about you and your race, that caused me to do what I did. Now, it is more. I would like your companionship—a concept which I did not know existed. I learned a word from your mind, the word *friend*."

"A word I thought I had forgotten," Crag said. "I want no friends. Let me alone."

"If you wish again to die—?"

Crag laughed. "Twice in one day? No, thank you. But how am I going to get back to Mars? You got me into this, damn you, by bringing me back to life. Now get me to Mars. Or get that spaceship back and I'll get there myself."

"I was afraid that would be your decision," said the voice. "The spaceship is already back, is orbiting about me right now. Shall I bring it down?"

"Yes," Crag said.

It bumped gently to the ground beside him and he stepped into the still open door, slammed it shut after him. He turned on the airmaker and, while giving it a chance to build up atmosphere so he could take off his space suit, sat down at the controls and started making the observations that would enable him to set a course back toward Mars. Without too much surprise he saw from the reflector for the down view port that the asteroid —or whatever it had been—was gone; he floated free in space.

Half an hour later, on course and with nothing to do until, two days later, he'd be nearing Mars, he relaxed and found himself wondering: Was he really sorry he'd been brought back to life? In a way, yes; he'd died once and that ought to be enough for any man, and dead men have no problems. On the other hand, he had half a million dollars, part of it on him in cash and the rest in banks back in Mars City, and it seemed a shame to die and leave it unspent. It was more money by far than he'd ever had at one time before; it would last him for years no matter how prodigally he spent it.

And why miss those years? Wasn't money what he wanted?

Or was it? He remembered those few minutes when he and Judeth had been alone, after Olliver's death and before hers—and then, with an oath, thrust the thought from his mind. He'd let himself get soft in those few minutes, but he didn't have to let himself stay that way.

"Good-by, Crag," said a voice in his ear, startling him.

He looked in all the viewports, saw nothing. "Where are you?" he asked.

"Where you left me. But in a few minutes you'll be out of my extreme range for doing this, so I thought I would tell you now what I have decided."

Crag said, "I don't care what you've decided. Let me alone; that's all I ask of you."

"I shall, but I want you to know my plans. I am going to make a world."

"All right, go ahead."

"Thank you." Crag thought the voice sounded amused. "I will. And you'll know about it when it happens. I think possibly you may decide to come to me. I'll wait and see."

"Don't hold your breath," Crag said. "All right, good-by." And then: "Wait, if you're still there. What the hell do you mean, you're going to make a world? You can't create matter, can you?"

"No need to. The matter is here—the millions of small and large asteroids in this belt between Mars and Jupiter. It *was* a planet once, a few million years ago, before it broke up. Some chunks of it have been lost, but there's still enough rock here to make a planet almost the size of Mars.

"All I have to do, Crag, is use myself as a nucleus for it and gather it together. And it will be a new world and a raw one; it'll need tough colonists. Crag, I hope you'll decide to gather some people like yourself, ones who are tough and not soft and weak like the others, to come to me. I want men who, like you, would not take orders even if I should give them. I do not want to be a god, Crag, even though I have some powers beyond mankind's; I would not let my new world be colonized by people who might even be tempted to obey me."

"Most people will—if you reward them. How are you going to keep them away?"

There was a sound that might have been laughter. "I'll take care of that, Crag. Whenever you're ready, come. And if you know any others besides yourself who are like you, bring them. I'll make them welcome."

Crag laughed. "I'll think it over—after I've spent that half million."

"That is all I ask. Good-by, Crag."

And suddenly there was a sense of emptiness in the spaceship and Crag knew that whatever projection of force and thought had been there was gone.

He was alone; suddenly it was a strange feeling, and it was strange that it should be strange for, in all the years he had been a criminal, he had been alone and had wanted to be alone. Was it because for those few minutes after Olliver's death and before Judeth's he had forgotten to hate her because they were both dying so hatred no longer helped or even mattered? Or was it because it was lonelier to have died and been brought back to life? Or was it because an alien mind had probed and shared his mind and now—*knew* him.

Another man, a character in mythology, had once died and been brought back to life, and had life ever again been the same for him? *Damn him,* he thought of the alien, the sentient rock; *why didn't he leave me alone? Isn't it enough for a man to die once?*

The two days it took him to get back to Mars seemed an interminable length of time. But he had to curb his impatience for at least a week longer than that if he wanted to be safe. It would have been very unwise to have landed Olliver's ship at Marsport or any other spaceport. The ship's papers, which would be checked, showed its last clearance had been from Mars City's Marsport with three abroad; it would have been impossible for him to have told any story to account for their disappearance that would not have led to an investigation, and an uncomfortable degree of official interest would have focused on Crag. Far better for the ship itself and all three of its occupants to be presumed never to have returned from space.

He landed the ship and lowered it to the horizontal position in the shadow of a high sand dune in the New Lybian desert; it might have been undiscovered there for years. But he took no chances; he walked—it took him four days—to the nearest town, a small mining community. There, claiming to be a prospector, he rented a sand-cat with a bulldozer attachment. It took him less than a day to drive back to the spaceship with it and another day to shift enough of the dune to cover the ship with sand. Another day to return to the mining town, return the sand-cat, and buy air passage to Mars City.

He was safe now. With his fingerprints and records destroyed, there was nothing left to connect him with the Crag who would be presumed dead along with Olliver and Judeth when, within another week, their spaceship would be reported missing and presumably lost, since a ship of its class carried supplies for two weeks at maximum loading—and that much only when there were two people aboard instead of three.

It was evening when he reached Mars City but all the shops were open, as were all the bars and everything else, twenty-four hours a day, so he was able to buy himself a complete new wardrobe and swanky luggage to put it in. He hadn't bothered to take his old luggage out of the spaceship; it wouldn't have fitted his new-found status of wealthy man.

Oddly, he was no longer in a hurry to begin his debauch. He was tired, for one thing; after his herculean labor in burying the spaceship, he needed a long sleep worse than he needed a drink. But he was in no hurry, even for that.

He asked the clerk from whom he had made his purchases, "What's the top luxury hotel now? Is it still the Luxor?"

"It's still the best one, I hear. There are a few newer ones in the last year, but none of them quite so expensive."

"Will you have the clothes packed in the luggage and sent there, right away?"

"Of course, Sir. But unless you have a reservation—?"

"Have them sent there," Craig said.

He went out of the shop. It was late evening by now, but the streets were as crowded as at noon. Mostly with expensively dressed men and women—and with people who didn't quite fit either category. Crag was expensively dressed himself now, in clothes he had changed into after he had bought them, although his costume was somber and modest compared to most of the others.

The Luxor was ten blocks away; the walk, he thought, might cure him of his restlessness and make him sleepy. But walking bored him; halfway there he decided to take a cab the rest of the way and then decided to stop in at a bar before he took the cab.

He put a bill on the bar and decided to start with a highball, an old-fashioned alcoholic drink that antedated by centuries the newer and more potent drug-based liquors. He sipped it slowly and wondered why he didn't feel exhilarated. He had what he'd always wanted—money, half a million dollars of it. And perfect safety; not only wasn't he wanted but his records and fingerprints had been expunged from criminal files everywhere.

He was simply tired, he thought. He'd feel better tomorrow.

And stared at himself in the backbar mirror; strange—or was it?—for how many centuries bars had had mirrors behind them so their patrons could stare at their own reflections—and reflect.

Crag stared at his own reflection, and reflected. I am Crag, he thought. But who was Crag, now? Crag had been someone, as a criminal. But now he was a rich man, one of millions of rich men, with no need to steal or kill, or to run or to hide. His only need was to enjoy himself, and he was making a bad start of it; the highball didn't taste right.

He puffed a cigarette into flame and inhaled deeply.

Someone was sitting beside him at the bar, a girl. She said. "May I have—?" and Crag handed her a cigarette. He didn't turn to face her, but in the mirror he could see that she had bronze hair the color of Judeth's and of his ex-wife's. But there was no further resemblance to either of them.

"Thanks, Mister," she said. "Would you buy me a drink, huh?"

He pushed a ten-dollar bill in front of her, from his change. "Buy one and keep the change. But please let me alone and don't talk."

It was cheap at the price. There were other prostitutes in the bar, a dozen or so of them, of both sexes. As long as she sat there, he'd be left alone; if she went away another would try, and another, and his thoughts would be interrupted each time. His thoughts? What had he been thinking about, anyway? Nothing.

He needed sleep; that was all that was wrong with him.

He looked down into his drink between sips because now if he looked into the mirror he'd see the girl sitting beside him, and the color of her hair would make him think about Judeth. But why shouldn't he think about Judeth if he wanted to? She was dead now, and he didn't need to be afraid of her any more. *Afraid?* How had that word come into his mind? He wasn't afraid of anything. What he had meant in his thoughts was that now he didn't need to hate her any longer.

Inadvertently he looked up and his eyes caught those of the girl, in the mirror. She said, " 'Scuse me for talking once, Mister. But you look lonesome. Aren't you? Or are you just mad at someone?"

Instead of answering Crag downed the rest of his drink and left. Outside, he started to hail a cab and then changed his mind and walked the rest of the way to the Luxor Hotel.

It was small compared to the buildings around it, only six stories high, but it was set back in the middle of a full city block of garden—all Earth trees, flowers and grass growing in soil brought from Earth, not the dull scrubby vegetation on Mars.

He walked back to it, and into the gilded and silvered lobby, across it to the polished marble desk.

"Got a suite open?" he asked. Nothing less than suites were available at the Luxor.

The desk clerk stared at him disdainfully through pince-nez glasses on a gray silk ribbon. His head was the shape of an egg, and as bald. "You have a reservation, Mr.—ah?"

"You have the name right," Crag said. "Mr. Ah. No, I haven't any reservation."

"Then there is nothing—"

"I'm a friend of the manager's," Crag said. "If you take my card in I'm sure something can be arranged." Crag put a hundred-dollar bill on the counter.

A corner of the man's mouth twitched, and his eyes warmed somewhat behind the pince-nez glasses; they became no colder than hailstones. He said, "*I* am the manager, Mr. Ah. My name is Carleton. But I could have erred; I'll check the register." He didn't touch the bill, but he brought up a crocodile-bound ledger from under the desk and covered the bill with it while he thumbed through pages.

After a moment he said, "Yes, there *is* a suite open, sir. Number Fourteen."

"Is it your best suite?"

"One of our best. Two hundred and thirty dollars a day."

"I'll take it," Crag said. He peeled bills off his roll and put them on the desk atop the open ledger. "You register for me, please. My luggage is being sent here but won't arrive until tomorrow. You can have it sent up when it arrives."

"Certainly, Mr. Ah." The manager touched a button and a bellboy sprang up as though by magic. "Suite Fourteen," he said, handing the boy a key.

In the thirty- by forty-foot beautifully furnished living room of the suite, Crag tipped the bellboy and assured him that he wanted nothing at the moment. He stood looking about him. Doors indicated that he had at least five other rooms at his disposal but before entering any of them he walked out on the balcony and stood a moment in the cool Martian night air looking out over the fabulously lighted streets and buildings that surrounded him. Quite a bit different from the spacemen's quarter, north of the city proper. But he was much safer here; in the luxury places like this one, no one who spent money freely was ever asked questions and it was almost impossible to get into trouble that you couldn't buy your way out of. If you threw money around they figured you were an important politician or a labor leader and expected you to be incognito as a matter of course.

He went back inside and tried a door. It led to a small but well-stocked bar. He studied the array of bottles and finally poured himself a small drink of *woji;* it would be more likely than any of the others to make him sleepy, and sleep was what he needed. It might even make him more cheerful. But its immediate effect seemed to be neither and it tasted bitter.

He went out into the main room and tried another door. It led to a library that was well stocked with books, records and tapes. He glanced over the books on the shelves, noticing that except for a few standard reference works that a traveler might want to refer to they were all pornographic; that meant that the tapes and records would be pornographic too. He didn't try any of them.

A double door in front of a pneumatic divan turned out to open on a video screen eight feet wide and six feet high. Crag turned on the switch and sat down on the divan. Bright colors flashed on the screen and settled into a picture, a musical show originating in London on Earth. Before a three-dimensional chorus undulating in full color a pale and slender tenor was singing:

Jet up! Jet down! On a slow ship to Venus!
Honey-wunny-bunny, how'd you like my . . .

Crag got up and turned off the switch. He went back and had another drink at the bar. This time he tried *estaquil*, one of the strongest of the hemp-derived drinks, supposed to be soothing and soporific. It tasted sickeningly sweet and seemed to have no effect on him otherwise.

He tried another door. It led to a room well supplied with gambling equipment of all kinds, one wall lined solid with solitaire gambling machines. Crag knew that all the machines would be rigged with high percentages against him and didn't bother trying them. Besides, what would be the fun in gambling when he already had more money than he knew what to do with. But one of the solitaire machines was an antique fifty-cent-piece one-arm bandit and Crag, for the hell of it and knowing that it would probably be set to pay off the first time, found a half dollar in his pocket, dropped it in and pulled the lever. The cylinders spun, one by one came to rest; a cherry, a cherry, an orange. Four half dollars clinked into the pay-off receptacle. Crag wandered on without bothering to take them out. He wandered back to the main salon and opened another door.

It led to the master bedroom, which was even larger than the living room or salon, whichever it was. It was much more richly furnished. Especially more richly furnished was the eight-foot-wide ebony bed; a blonde, a brunette and a redhead, all naked, lay upon it. For a second Crag thought that the redhead looked a little like Judeth, but she didn't.

She was the one, though, that caught his eye. She sat up and raised her arms above her head, stretching like a kitten as she smiled at him. "Hello," she said. The other two sat up and smiled at him too.

Crag leaned against the jamb of the door. He said, "Pardon my ignorance, but I've never had a suite here before. Are you standard equipment?"

The redhead laughed. "Of course. But you needn't keep *all* of us, unless you wish." She looked demurely at her gilded toenails.

The blonde smiled at him and then rolled over on her back, obviously figuring she showed to better advantage that way. She did.

The brunette gave him a gamin grin. "We're more fun three at a time," she said. "We know tricks."

Crag said, "Get out, all of you."

They didn't argue; they didn't even seem offended or annoyed. They got up calmly and went past him through the doorway of the bedroom and through the salon, through the door to the hallway, still stark naked but obviously completely unconcerned about the fact.

Crag laughed. He went back to the bar and poured himself another drink. Plain whiskey this time. Since none of the drinks tasted right to him just now, he might as well vary them.

He sat sipping it, trying not to think.

There was a soft knock at the door. Crag put down his glass and went to answer it. His luggage, probably, although he hadn't expected it so soon; he'd told the clerk at the store that there was nothing he'd need tonight and that delivery tomorrow would be satisfactory.

But the bellboy outside his door didn't have luggage. He was a very beautiful young man, rosy and handsome, with soft ringlets of curly hair.

He smiled at Crag. "The management sent me, Sir. Since you did not want women, they thought perhaps— Is there anything I can do for you?"

Crag looked him over carefully. He said, "Turn around."

The young man smiled knowingly and turned gracefully around. He had a pleasingly plump posterior; he wriggled it a trifle, provocatively.

Crag drew back his foot and kicked hard.

He closed the door gently.

He got the glass of whiskey again and downed what was left of it instead of sipping. He started wandering again, wondering why he couldn't get sleepy. He found another and smaller bedroom, but this one was untenanted. And he found the bathroom, with a sunken tub that was almost large enough to swim in. The tub was filled with lukewarm water and Crag stripped and got in.

But he got out quickly when he discovered that the water was perfumed. He finished washing himself with cold but unperfumed water from the tap of the washbasin. And then washed himself all over again when he found that he still smelled faintly of violets.

He put his shorts back on to sleep in—if he could sleep —and went into the master bedroom. But a look at the monstrous ebony bed there changed his mind; he went into the smaller bedroom and lay down on the smaller and less ornate bed there. Probably unspeakable things had happened on it too, but fewer of them. He turned out the light and tried to sleep.

But couldn't. He wondered if there was a drug cabinet in the liquor room. He didn't use drugs as such ordinarily, but he had to sleep. If he didn't he'd start drinking seriously and a time when he was dead tired already was a bad time to start that.

He wondered if music would help. He'd noticed knobs and luminous dials of a radio built into the wall above the head of the bed and he reached up now and flicked the switch. The radio hummed and then blared; he got it turned down to a bearable volume just in time to catch the end of a news broadcast.

". . . in the asteroid belt," said a smooth voice. "Scientists of both Mars and Earth are working on the problem, but have thus far failed to formulate an acceptable theory to account for the unprecedented and incredible phenomenon. This concludes the two o'clock newscast; the next one will be presented at 3:15 A.M. Mars City time."

Crag sat up and turned the light back on. He shut off

the radio and reached for the phone beside the bed. An obsequious voice asked him to wait for a moment and then came the dry voice of the manager with the pince-nez glasses. "Carleton speaking. Yes, Mr. Ah?"

Crag said, "I just tuned in on the last few sentences of a newscast from the official Mars City station. About something happening in the asteroid belt. Could you arrange with the station to have that particular part of the newscast played back for me over my set here?"

"I'm afraid, Mr. Ah, that would require rewiring the set; it is automatically tuned to the main carrier wave of—"

"Over this phone, then," Crag said. "They tape all broadcasts; for a fee they ought to be willing to play that part of the tape back for me."

"I'll see if that can be arranged, Sir. If you'll please cradle your phone I'll call you back as soon as I've found out what arrangement can be made."

Crag cradled the phone and drew a cigarette into flame while he waited. In a few minutes the phone buzzed and he picked it up again.

"It can be done, Mr. Ah. There will be a fee of fifty dollars. Is that satisfactory?"

"Yes. Hurry it up or I might as well wait till the next newscast."

"Very well. If you'll please hang up again—"

Crag put down the phone again and watched it, wondering now why he was so interested and in such a hurry. Whatever was going on out in the asteroid belt didn't concern him. If the alien out there was doing what he'd said he'd do, that still meant nothing to Crag. A new world, hell. For as long as his money lasted—and half a million dollars takes a lot of spending—he was going to enjoy a soft life here on a soft world, not help start a colony of criminals on a new, raw planet.

But just the same he watched the phone with mounting impatience until it buzzed for a second time.

"The station is ready, Sir. The management of the Luxor is glad to have been able to arrange—"

"Get off the wire, then," Crag said.

There was another minute of waiting and then came the voice of the announcer of the newscast.

"According to many reliable reports, a strange and incredible thing is happening in the asteroid belt. The first report came eight hours ago from Bellini, an astronomer who was at that time using the big scope on Luna to observe Ceres—largest of the asteroids, with a diameter of four hundred and eighty miles—when suddenly it vanished from the field of the scope, which had been set to track it, to follow its course automatically. When Bellini found it again by using the manual controls, it had changed both speed and direction considerably. The directional change was quickly analyzed by the computing machine and it was found that Ceres had lost much of the eccentric and parabolic aspect of its orbit; it was following a new orbit, more nearly regular and more nearly in the plane of the ecliptic. Subsequent observations fed into the computer showed that the change is progressive, and still continues. Within another forty hours, Bellini believes, Ceres will be following a perfectly circular orbit about the sun instead of the irregular one it followed heretofore.

"Luna immediately notified other observatories on Earth and on Mars and those in a position to observe Ceres confirmed his observations within the hour. Also, observations were made and are still being made, of other of the asteroids, those large enough to be observable in telescopes. Hidalgo, whose eccentricity is—or rather was —point six five, was found with difficulty, considerably out of its former orbit. Upon study and analysis with the computer, it too was found changing in the direction of a perfectly circular orbit similar to that of Ceres—but Hidalgo is traveling at a far greater speed; it will overtake and crash into Ceres within a few days.

"The most amazing thing is that the speed of the asteroid Hidalgo in its new orbit and in relation to its mass is impossible according to the laws of angular momentum.

"Luna Observatory is now on the wrong side of Earth to enable continued observation of the asteroid belt, but every telescope on the night sides of Earth and Mars is now being used to check one asteroid after another—and as yet no single one has been found which is in its former orbit! All are now in, or tending toward the same identical circular orbit. And there is only one conclusion to be drawn—since they are moving at greatly different speeds, they will eventually all crash into one another *and form a new planet!*

"If it can be assumed that the smaller asteroids, those too tiny to be seen telescopically, are joining in this movement then the new planet about to be formed will be slightly larger than Mars.

"Spaceships are now leaving Mars and Earth to place themselves near enough to observe this incredible development at close hand. Whatever its cause, an event of cosmic importance is taking place in the asteroid belt. Scientists of both Mars and Earth are working on the problem, but have thus far failed to formulate an acceptable theory to account for . . ."

Crag put the phone back on its cradle; that was the point at which he'd tuned in on the original broadcast ten or fifteen minutes before.

He thought, *So the little devil is really doing it.*

He chuckled and went back to the bar where he poured himself another drink, *woji* again this time. With it in his hand he wandered out onto the dark balcony and stood staring up at the moon Phobos hurtling across the Martian sky.

Then he stared at the stars until he had located the plane of the ecliptic and knew that he was looking at the belt in which the asteroids—each too small to be seen by the naked eye at this distance—were gathering themselves, or being gathered, to form a new planet. He chuckled again, but there was no real mirth in it.

He raised his fist at the sky and thought, *Damn you, I died; why didn't you leave me dead? Once is enough.*

He drank his bitter drink and threw the glass out over the railing into the garden below.

And then staggered, not from intoxication but from exhaustion, back into the smaller bedroom, fell upon the bed, and slept.

▼▼▼▼▼▼▼▼▼▼▼▼▼▼▼▼▼▼▼▼▼▼▼▼▼▼▼▼▼▼▼▼

CHAPTER EIGHT

CRAG woke, as always, suddenly and completely, instantly oriented. He was in his own suite at the Luxor, in the smaller of two bedrooms, and the dimness of the light coming in from outside didn't confuse him; he knew that it was dusk, not dawn, and that he'd slept fourteen or fifteen hours.

He sat up on the edge of the bed and got a cigarette going, then he wandered out into the salon. His luggage, he saw, had arrived and had been brought to his suite, left just inside the door so its arrival would not disturb him. He carried it into the bedroom and opened it, chose garments and put them on.

He felt rested. Today was the day, or rather tonight was the night, when he was going to start a historic binge, the binge he'd worked for and waited for.

But he was hungry; he'd better eat first. Once he'd started drinking he wouldn't eat until after he'd sobered up again, however long that might be. He considered having food sent up and then decided to go downstairs for it. The dining room of the Luxor was always open and served any kind of meal at any hour of the day, with a floor show every hour on the hour, twenty-four times a day. He was curious what the floor show would be.

A voice called, "Mr. Ah," as he was passing the desk. Crag turned and saw it was Carleton, the manager. He stopped and rested an elbow on the desk.

"May I ask how long you are staying, Mr. Ah?"

"I don't know," Crag said. "A few more days at least. Maybe forever."

"I see. I'm afraid, then, that I must ask you to pay for a second day. And besides smaller items, there are already two fifty-dollar debits against your account—"

Crag put a thousand-dollar bill on the desk. "Let me know when that's used up. One fifty-dollar charge is for the newscast repeat. What's the other?"

"A fee to the bellboy we sent to your room last night. You—ah—used his services in an unusual way, but what you did incapacitated him for a day and we thought it only fair—"

"Only fair," said Crag solemnly. "And well worth it."

He turned away but the manager's "Mr.—ah—Ah," made him turn back.

"The Luxor regrets that you did not care for the girls. Or for the bellboy, in the ordinary way. But we deem it a privilege to serve guests with extraordinary tastes. We can supply children of either sex, elderly people . . . If, as your treatment of the boy might indicate, you prefer satisfaction through the infliction of pain, we have a choice selection of very special equipment. And people in all categories who are willing, at a price, to submit to —ah—whatever you prefer."

"*Any* category?" Crag asked.

"Any, Sir. The Luxor prides itself on being able to please."

Crag said, "I like hotel managers. You might drop up yourself sometimes. And bring a corkscrew."

He walked into the dining room. A girl in a costume so abbreviated as to be almost nonexistent met him smilingly, led him to a table and took his order for a drink. He looked around and saw that all the waitresses were similarly undressed, and wondered vaguely what the floor show could offer to distract attention from the waitresses. Then the floor show started, and he saw. After a while he got up in disgust and walked out of the dining room and out of the hotel. A few blocks away he found a restaurant that specialized in food instead of sex; he ordered a big meal and ate it.

Then, over a cigarette and a brandy, he wondered if he should go back to the Luxor only long enough to get the change from his thousand-dollar bill and pick up his luggage. But he decided not to; any hotel in Mars City would be almost as bad if it was big enough and luxurious enough to provide the kind of quarters he wanted. And by now he probably had enough of a reputation at the Luxor that he'd be left alone as long as he stayed in his own suite. The door had a good solid bolt that he could use and privacy was all he wanted for his binge. He could, of course, go to a cheap hotel like the one he'd stayed in the night before he'd taken off with Olliver for the asteroid belt, but a single cheap room would be depressing and since he had so much money he might as well have the best quarters he could buy, even if he wasn't interested in all the sex and other vice—except drinking—offered with it.

What good was money if he didn't spend it?

Or maybe that was what was wrong with him, the fact that he *had* money. A criminal with money is an unemployed man, with nothing in life to interest him—until he's spent it and again has incentive to start casing another job. Maybe he should throw or gamble the money away and start working again. But that was ridiculous; he'd have admitted to himself that the new money he'd be working for would be worthless to him too. He'd be admitting to himself that he not only had no reason for stealing, but none for living.

Well, *did* he have?

There was only one answer to that, and it was to get drunk, so what was he waiting for?

He went back to the Luxor and to his suite; he put out the "Do Not Disturb" sign and bolted the door.

He went to the bar and started getting drunk. Slowly— he didn't want to knock himself out right away; he wanted to enjoy the drinking—but very thoroughly. Dawn found him still at it, pacing like a caged tiger up and down the salon with a glass in his hand. But not staggering, never spilling a drop, except down his throat. Drunk but under control, not blind drunk or raging drunk.

Only once had he interrupted himself, an hour before when the bar's supply of *woji* had run out. He was on a *woji* binge and didn't want to switch drinks so phoned down to the desk and asked that a case of it be sent up to restock the bar. But he hadn't wanted to see anyone or have anyone see him, so he'd unlocked the door and taken down the sign and then had gone into the bathroom and taken a shower. When he'd dressed and come out again the liquor was there. He'd relocked the door, put back the sign and started drinking again.

It was noon when he reached the stage of violence. He smashed gambling equipment, broke bottles, kicked in the eight-foot-wide television screen.

After that, he slept a while, woke feeling horrible and started drinking again. He lost track of time. Whenever he slept he had no way of knowing whether it was for a few minutes or for many hours. Nor could he even guess—or care about—the lengths of the periods when he drank. Sometimes it was light and sometimes it was dark, and neither mattered.

Nothing mattered except staying drunk and not thinking.

But not thinking about what? His mind shied away from that. Besides, he still hated her; the fact that she was dead couldn't change that. She was, or had been, a woman.

Then came the time when he awakened feeling nauseated and weak, and he knew the binge was over. He sat up on the edge of the bed—the one in the smaller bedroom—and picked up the phone, asked the day and the hour. He'd been drunk four days; again it was early evening, as it had been when he'd started his drinking. He made it to the bathroom and was sick. After that he felt better; he showered, shaved and put on clean clothes.

He looked around the suite and guessed the damage he'd done at close to a thousand dollars, which probably meant they'd charge him twice that. Which didn't matter; maybe the sooner his half million was gone the better. He'd have to figure ways of spending money; thus far he'd hardly made a dent in it.

Maybe gambling would be the answer, if he could find an honest game so he could enjoy it. But finding an honest gambling game in Mars City—or in most other places in the system—was almost as hard as finding an honest woman. Maybe there wasn't any such thing. There was no honesty anywhere, not only not in gambling or women, but not in politics, business or anything else.

He went downstairs, and stopped at the desk. Carleton, the manager, wasn't on duty, but Crag told the clerk that a hurricane had struck his suite and that the hotel should make repairs immediately and bill him for them. He'd be gone a few hours and wanted the suite ready for use again when he got back. The clerk told him, "Yes, Sir."

He walked to the restaurant where he'd last eaten four days ago. He wasn't hungry but he forced himself to eat a fair meal and felt better. Only his mind still felt dull.

Walking, and the cool Martian night air, would cure that. And perhaps, now that he'd eaten, one pick-up drink. Besides, he had to kill time before going back to the hotel unless he wanted to be there while they were repairing or replacing the things he'd smashed.

He walked. Across the night and across the city he walked, and felt his mind clearing and his strength returning. He hated weakness, in himself or anyone else but especially in himself.

He passed a good many bars before he chose one for his pick-up drink, a plain simple bar that might have come out of the old days of a few centuries before. And was pleased when he entered it to see that he'd guessed right; there were no women there, and no homosexuals. Besides a bartender there were only two customers in the place, seated together at a table sipping drinks and talking quietly together.

Crag crossed to the bar and took a stool. The big lantern-jawed bartender moved down the bar opposite him without speaking. Crag ordered his drink and got it, having momentary trouble finding a bill small enough for a small bar like this one to be able to cash. He remembered he was trying to spend money, not to save it, and told the bartender to have a drink with him.

The bartender thanked him and poured a second drink. He reached behind him and flicked the switch of a radio. "May be a newscast on," he said.

There was, but it was a political discussion; the announcer was discussing probabilities and possibilities in the coming elections—just as though he meant what he was saying, as though he didn't know that there weren't any possibilities or probabilities, that the results of elections had already by now been decided in closed conferences between the leaders of the two big parties and that the casting and counting of votes was only a formality.

Crag said a four-letter word and the lantern-jawed bartender nodded. "Yeah, it's hogwash," he said. " I was hoping there'd be something on the new planet, but that would have been at the start of the 'cast. Well, I heard the report on it a couple hours ago; guess there hasn't anything much happened since then." He reached back to turn off the radio and then stayed his hand.

The newscaster was saying: "From Earth. The great Judge Olliver is reported missing in space. Olliver's private spaceship, a J-14 class ship, cleared from Mars City two weeks ago, presumably to return to Earth. Olliver was accompanied by his wife and his personal pilot. The ship has not been reported as landing on Earth or elsewhere, and since it carried supplies for three people for a period not to exceed ten days, it can only be presumed that . . ."

"Hell," he said, "that's one guy in politics who *might* have been straight. Say, what's your idea on this new planet business?"

"I haven't any," Crag said. "What's yours?"

"Damn if I know. Why should I, when even the science boys ain't got an idea what's going on. Oh, they got theories; they always got theories. But none of them makes any sense. The one thing they can't admit is that something goes on they can't understand. 'Nother drink?"

Crag said, "Thanks, no. I'm leaving now."

He got down off the stool and started for the door. There was a click and Crag recognized the sound and its source and reacted instantaneously; he saved his life by dropping so fast that the shot missed him. The click had been the lock of the door he'd been walking toward and it had been electrically activated from behind the bar.

The place was a deadfall, as some small quiet bars were, especially ones near the outskirts of a big city, as this one was. In such a place, a solitary customer didn't leave alive if he was foolish enough to be well dressed and to flash a roll of big denomination bills, as Crag had. He saw now, even as he fell, that the two customers who'd been seated at the table when he'd entered were no longer there; they'd happened to leave quietly while he'd been listening to the newscast or to the bartender.

The second drink the bartender had just asked him if he'd wanted would, no doubt, have been a poisoned one. Since he'd turned it down and started for the door, the bartender had fallen back upon his second line of offense; he'd activated the lock of the outer door by remote control and had picked up and used a weapon he'd had ready behind the bar.

The weapon, Crag could see now, from the floor, was an antique sawed-off shotgun, still—if you didn't mind noise, and this bar like most was doubtless soundproofed —as dangerous a weapon as existed for close or medium range shooting. It was being lowered now, the bartender was trying to line it up on Crag again before he pulled the second trigger.

But Crag was rolling fast toward the bar and close enough to it now so the gun couldn't aim at him, unless the bartender climbed up on the bar. And running footsteps behind the bar told Crag that the bartender was coming around the end of the bar—and which end he was coming around. Crag sat up, facing that way, his metal left hand gripped in his good right one, and his right arm cocked to throw.

It scored a bull's-eye in the bartender's face as he came around the end and before he could even begin to aim the shotgun.

That was the end of the fight; it had lasted less than three seconds, and the bartender was dead.

Crag got back his hand and dusted himself off. He

went back of the bar to the cash register and found a little more than a hundred dollars. But in the bartender's pocket he found proof that the man had made a good haul, and recently. There were eight thousand-dollar bills. Crag grimaced, and then laughed at himself for doing so. He was getting ahead of the game instead of behind; his total expenditures out of the half million, even counting the damage to his suite for which he'd not yet paid, would be less than the eight thousand he'd just found.

Rather than risk being seen leaving the place, he left by a back door into an alley.

Back at the hotel a clerk, not the manager, was on duty at the desk. But he told Crag that the damage in his suite was repaired and presented him a bill. The bill was only slightly higher than Crag had guessed it would be; he paid it, and another thousand in advance.

"Thank you, Mr. Ah," the clerk said. "If there is anything—?"

There wasn't anything else he wanted, Crag assured him.

In his suite, he wandered around for a while and then turned on the radio in the salon; it was a few minutes before the hour and there would be a newscast on the hour. He suffered through a commercial and then sat down as the newscaster started talking.

"First the latest reports on the new planet forming in the asteroid belt—or in what was the asteroid belt.

"The planet is forming with incredible rapidity. It is estimated that nine tenths of all the former asteroids are now a part of it. It is currently approximately the size and mass of Mars, and will be slightly larger when the remaining free asteroids have crashed into it—as, within another four to six hours all of them will have done. Those behind it in its orbit are accelerating speed so they will crash into it; those ahead of it in its orbit are decelerating and it will overtake them.

"The planet is revolving, but the period of revolution, even if it has as yet stabilized, cannot be determined until the clouds of dust thrown up by the crashing of the arriving asteroids have settled sufficiently to make the surface visible. The fact that this dust stays suspended in clouds is proof that the new planet, incredible as this may seem, already has an atmosphere. Because of the thickness of the dust an accurate spectroscopic examination cannot be made as yet, but the atmosphere definitely contains oxygen and will probably be breathable.

"Observations, spectroscopic and otherwise, are now being made from spaceships only a few hundred thousand miles away. Landings and exploration will be made as soon as the solar council deems them to be safe.

"No decision has been made yet on a name for the new planet. Majority opinion favors giving the honor of naming it to Bellini, the astronomer who, through the big scope on Luna, first observed the perturbation of the orbit of the asteroid Ceres. His report focused attention upon the asteroid belt and led to the discovery of what was happening there."

The newscast switched to politics and Crag shut it off.

He wondered if there might be a picture of the new planet on video; surely they'd be scanning it from the ships out there observing from so relatively close. He opened the double doors behind which was the big video screen, flicked the switch and backed away from it while it warmed up.

The set hummed and brilliant colors flashed on the screen; then the hum turned into music—if one could call it that—and the colors became a larger-than-life closeup of a beautiful young man with blond ringlets of hair, plucked eyebrows and full sensuous lips that were crooning:

> Jet up! Jet down! On a slow ship to Venus!
> Honey-wunny-bunny . . .

Calmly and soberly, without anger, Crag walked to the screen and kicked it in.

He went to the bar and poured himself a short nightcap, found himself yawning before he finished drinking it, and went to bed as soon as he'd finished it.

And dreamed, but in the morning did not remember any of the things he had dreamed. Which was just as well, for being Crag he would have been disgusted with himself for having dreamed them.

The next day he spent walking, refamiliarizing himself with the downtown business section of Mars City. He went to the two banks at which he'd left part of his money before leaving Mars with Olliver a couple of weeks before. He'd left it there because he hadn't trusted Olliver. But he didn't trust the banks either and decided now that he'd rather have his money in cash. True, there was a chance of his being killed and robbed, as he had almost been last night, but if he was killed it might as well be for a large sum as a relatively small one; whatever was left wasn't going to do him any good.

But he found that he had failed to realize how bulky half a million would be. Even with most of it in tenthousand-dollar bills, the largest denomination available except for banking transactions, it made a stack of bills an inch thick. Even divided among several pockets he found it awkward to carry. So that evening he hid most of it in his suite, a hundred thousand dollars in each of four caches. He used ingenuity and imagination in finding those caches in places where it was almost impossible for them to be found, even by a person deliberately searching.

It killed the evening for him.

▼▼▼▼▼▼▼▼▼▼▼▼▼▼▼▼▼▼▼▼▼▼▼▼▼▼▼▼▼▼▼▼▼▼▼▼▼▼

CHAPTER NINE

HE WENT out again the next day and found himself gravitating into the spacemen's quarter, which was just north of the main downtown district. Spacemen did hang out there—especially when they were broke or nearly broke—but they made up only a small fraction of the floating population. In character it was a tenderloin district, a Skid Row.

Crag had no business going there, he knew, for the quarter offered nothing that he couldn't have obtained elsewhere—and much more safely. In the quarter, murders, fights and robberies were everyday matters, and the police went in squads of six; they were hated so much that a lone policeman wouldn't have survived a day. Let alone a night.

Yes, it was a dangerous district for a man who was dressed expensively and was carrying almost a hundred thousand dollars in cash. Maybe that was why Crag liked it. Danger stimulated him, made him alert and alive. Only in danger of death did he find joy in life.

Was it because, he sometimes wondered, subconsciously death was what he really wanted? Was his hatred of humanity so great, and his loneliness so great that he could find happiness only in oblivion?

Sometimes he thought so, and at least casually contemplated the simple and obvious answer. *Nephthin* would do it. *Nepthin* was difficult to obtain, but anything could be obtained if you knew the ropes and had plenty of money. Even *nephthin,* the one drug that drug peddlers hated as much as policemen did. There was no future in selling *nephthin* because it didn't build any repeat trade; you could sell only one dose to a customer because it killed him within twenty hours. It put him into a state of ecstasy for a while that was more intense by a hundred times than any other drug could achieve, and then put him in a berserker rage in which he went out and killed as many people as he could before being killed himself. If he wasn't killed, if he was caught and restrained instead, he died just the same—but still in ecstasy, no matter what was being done to him. It was a perfect finish for a man who wanted, for whatever reason, to go out in a blaze of ecstatic glory, especially if he hated people and liked the idea of taking a few, or a dozen, of them along with him, so it was understandable why the sale or even the possession of *nephthin* had been legislated to be a crime punishable by nothing less than twenty years' labor on Callisto, or the psycher. Even most hardened criminals and dope peddlers took a dim view of it—unless they themselves felt inclined to sample its pleasures, in which case of course they had nothing to lose.

But oddly although he would be perfectly content to be dead (and can the dead be otherwise than content?), Crag had no active desire to die. Not, at least, by his own hand.

He remembered a book, a very old one that he had read once, about the hunting of tigers in a part of Earth once known as India; it had told of a killer tiger, a maneater, which had terrorized an Indian province for years and killed hundreds of people. To the terrified natives it had been known as "The Moaner" because of the sound it made constantly when it prowled near a village at night. When a white hunter, the author of the book, finally killed it, he had examined the tiger and found a very old and deep-seated infection; the bone was decayed and the flesh around it rotten and pulpy. For years every step the tiger had taken had been excruciating agony, yet he had prowled and killed and eaten. Tigers don't commit suicide, not even with *nephthin*.

Crag tried gambling, but there wasn't much in it for him. The big games, like the ones in the gambling rooms of the Luxor, were so ridiculously crooked that there was no point, no enjoyment, in bucking them. He might as well have made a bonfire of the money and enjoyed its warmth. He went to the Luxor's main gambling salon once, but only once, the second day after he'd finished his drinking binge. For a while he drew cards in a *mara* game at a hundred dollars a card and managed to lose a few thousand dollars but the dealing was so obviously sleight of hand that finally, in utter disgust, he slapped his metal hand down, not too hard, on the hand of the dealer who was passing him a card. The dealer screamed and dropped two cards where only one should have been, and then stepped back whimpering to nurse his broken hand. Crag walked out, wondering whether the hotel would bill him for *that*. But the hotel didn't; too many people had seen that extra card.

For a while he gambled in Spacetown dives. Honest games could be found there, if one looked hard enough. But spacemen and the hangers-on of Spacetown aren't rich enough to play for high stakes and, after a while, low-stake play bored Crag because it didn't matter whether he won or lost.

He drank a lot, but not too much at any one time or place, never letting himself get out of control. The go-for-drunk kind of drinking was something Crag did only rarely and after a long period of abstinence, enforced or otherwise. He never drank while he was working on a job, or in space, but if the job or the trip took a long time he made up for it afterwards. Ordinarily he drank steadily but never to excess.

He did most of his drinking in Spacetown and found himself using the bar in his Luxor suite only for a first drink each morning and a final one each night. He considered taking a room in Spacetown—which had no luxury hotels, but a few fairly nice ones—but decided against it. Knowing full well that it was ridiculous of him to keep so expensive a suite when he made so little use of it, he still kept it. It cost money and when he faced things frankly he admitted to himself that the sooner he got rid of his money the less unhappy he'd be. While it lasted he had no reason for stealing more, and he was out of work.

He was like a tiger shut in an abattoir, surrounded by meat he doesn't have to hunt for. He can sate himself and keep himself sated, but pretty soon he comes to wish he was back in the jungle where the hunt and the kill comes before the feast. A sated tiger is only part a tiger, but still it does not kill for wanton enjoyment. A criminal with all the money he needs is no longer a criminal, but unless he is psychopathic he does not plot to get more.

Nor, unless he is psychopathic, does he deliberately throw away the money he has simply to restore his incentive. Because by doing so he negates to himself the value of money so no future sum of it would be worth having either, and willy-nilly destroys his incentive, his raison d'être, just as effectively.

No, the only thing Crag could do with the money was to *spend* it, and continuing to live at the Luxor was a help in that direction.

Too bad he'd never been interested in wealth per se, or in power. But he'd never considered money as other than something to spend, and power meant politics and he'd always hated politics, even before he'd become a criminal.

There were newscasts, of course. He never used the set in his suite any more but from time to time he couldn't avoid hearing or seeing the latest news on a set operating in whatever bar he happened to be in at the time.

On one of his early trips into Spacetown he was sitting in a small bar, one that was a bit more crowded than he liked although he had plenty of elbow room as he sat on the bar and stared into his glass of *woji*.

Suddenly the bartender flicked a switch under the bar and a radio blared into music, if you could call it music.

Crag reached across the bar and touched the man's arm. "Shut it off," he said.

The bartender met his gaze. "Mister, you ain't the only one in here. Some of them like that stuff and want it."

"I don't," Crag said, and his touch on the man's arm turned into a grip. "Shut it off."

The bartender winced and his eyes, looking into Crag's, saw something there that changed his tone of voice. He said, "Mister, I'll turn it down, but that's the best I can do. Guy down at the other end of the bar told me to turn it on and *he'll* make trouble if I turn it off. I don't know how tough you are, but he's plenty tough, as tough as they come in Mars City or anywhere else. You might make trouble if I leave it on, but I know damn well he'll mop up the place with me if I turn it off."

The bartender gently massaged his arm where Crag's hand had held it. He said hopefully, "Unless you and him want to go outside and settle it. Then I can obey whichever of you comes back in."

Crag grinned. He'd have enjoyed nothing better but he remembered he was getting into as few fights as possible these days and that anyway in this case he didn't have sufficient cause to start one.

"All right," he said. "Turn it down."

If the tough guy objected to that, then—

The bartender cut the volume to about half of what it had been. Then he said, "There's only another minute or two of that crap and then a newscast comes on. I think it's the newscast Gardin wanted me to turn it on for anyway. So what the hell."

Crag agreed, so what the hell.

He glanced toward the other end of the bar and had no difficulty in picking out which of the several men there was the one the bartender had called Gardin. There was only one of them who looked hard enough to scare a bartender. The others were space kids, cadets barely in their twenties. Gardin was more nearly like Crag, medium in size but compact, almost stocky but with a subtle suggestion of grace as well as strength. He was a little younger than Crag but not much, and he had black hair as against Crag's blond. Like Crag, he was a criminal, but the stamp of criminality showed much more obviously on him than it ever had on Crag.

The newscast came on but Crag, thinking his own thoughts, didn't hear the first part of it. But then, whether he wanted to or not, he found himself unable not to listen when the words "the new planet" penetrated his conciousness.

". . . still shrouded in clouds of dust, but they seem to be thinning. However, Admiral Yates has forbidden any attempt at landing until the surface is visible from space. The landing expedition is standing by, ready, but it may be weeks before . . . many mysterious features, not least of which is the fact that the amount of heat radiation is entirely too high for a planet so far out from the sun; the new planet will have approximately the same temperatures and seasons as Earth, despite the fact that it is more than twice Earth's mean distance from the sun. The difference, most scientists believe, is from internal heat generated by the impact of the asteroids when they came together. . . . *All* asteroids have now crashed into and become part of this new body; there is no loose matter of any size revolving in what was once the orbit of the asteroids and is now the orbit of the new planet.

"Current estimate of its diameter is six thousand miles, about halfway between the diameter of Mars and that of Earth. Density about five times that of water, almost the same as the density of Earth. Its gravity will be a little less than Earth's . . . definitely revolving but exact rate of revolution cannot be determined until the dust clouds settle and observations can be made of a fixed point on its surface . . .

"Pardon me for a second. I am being handed a bulletin . . .

"Big news, friends. The new planet has been named. Bellini of Luna Observatory, who was by acclamation of his fellow astronomers given the privilege of naming the new planet, has just announced his choice. He explains that he did not adopt a name out of mythology, since just about every mythological name was used up in naming the thousands of asteroids large enough to have been named, and he does not believe it a good idea to name the new body as a whole after any one of the smaller bodies which came together to comprise it.

"He chose therefore an arbitrary but euphonious combination of syllables, and has named the new planet—here it comes folks—Cragon. Spelled C-r-a-g-o-n—Cragon . . ."

Crag was leaning backward, holding onto the edge of the bar, roaring with laughter. It was the loudest, most sincere laughter he'd ever had since—since he could remember. *The little devil,* he thought. *The little devil got into an astronomer's mind and named himself after me. He thinks he's going to get me that way!*

There was a light tap on his shoulder and he quit laughing and turned around.

Gardin stood there, his face impassive but managing to look like a tightly coiled spring. He said, "Were you laughing at me, friend?"

Crag's laughter subsided, but he still chuckled slightly. "No," he said, "I wasn't. But I'll be glad to if you want me to, if it can lead to fun and games."

Gardin gestured to the bartender. "Shut it off," he said. And the radio, which was now playing music, clicked into silence.

"What *were* you laughing at?" Gardin asked gently.

Crag's eyes cooled, but not too cold. He said, "Something that's my business and too complicated to explain. But—say something funny, will you?"

Suddenly Gardin laughed too. "There isn't anything funny, is there? All right, I was off base. Forget it."

Crag said, "Unless you want to go outside, for laughs—"

"You had your laugh, whatever it was. I'll get by without. How's about a drink instead?"

"Sure," Crag said.

And he'd made a friend, or as near to a friend as he'd ever allowed himself to have.

He never learned anything about Gardin's past, but of course Gardin didn't learn anything about Crag's either.

They didn't trust one another that far. At first they didn't trust one another at all, but time took care of that. Time and the fact that mounting evidence convinced each that the other wasn't on the make, at the moment. If Gardin had been broke. . . .

But Gardin obviously wasn't broke; there was plenty of evidence for that. He was holing up, enjoying and spending a big haul. And being restless about it, too. Wanting action.

He knew these things about Gardin, as he knew Gardin knew these things about him. Oh, there were differences too; they weren't peas from a pod. Crag thought he was stronger, physically and mentally. But they never tested, or thought of testing, their physical strength. And mental strength—or will power or guts or whatever you want to call it—is something that only unexpected emergency or danger tests.

And in another way Gardin was different. He had a woman. He never mentioned whether she was his wife or not—which wouldn't have mattered to Crag in any case—but from things said from time to time, Crag gathered that they'd been together for several years. Her name was Bea, and she was a big brassy blonde. Crag found himself able to get along with her because she was so definitely someone else's property and so definitely a one-man woman. She left Crag strictly alone, the times the three of them were together. Whether this was because she was afraid of Gardin Crag didn't know, and didn't care; he did take care not to find out by ever being with her when Gardin wasn't around.

When Bea was with the two of them, Crag could almost forget that she was a woman. She drank and swore with them on equal terms, dressed modestly—for Mars City—and never coquetted, even with Gardin, when Crag was around. What they did when he wasn't around he managed not to think about.

Mostly Crag and Gardin wandered alone, although occasionally Bea went with them. Neither of them asked the other where he lived, or cared. There were places where they came to frequent when they felt like seeing one another, and that was enough.

For a while they found enjoyment—or surcease—in gambling with one another, head-to-head poker, *maraja*, and other games that two can play with a borrowed deck of cards in a quiet back room of a bar with no kibitzers. For a while the games ran even, and got higher. But then, as they got higher, Crag found himself winning more and more often. He knew Gardin well enough by then to be able to read subtleties of expression and manner well enough to know when to be cautious and when to plunge.

And suddenly he had about eighty thousand dollars of Gardin's money in front of him and suddenly he knew by the tiny signs that showed through the calm outwardness of Gardin's face, that Gardin was hurting, was going broke. And that quite likely the stake Gardin and Bea were living on was more likely in the neighborhood of a hundred thousand than half a million. And Crag didn't want their money; he had enough troubles of his own. Carefully he started losing, not so suddenly as to be obvious and not all in one game. But when they were back about even, several games later, he lost interest in gambling. And so did Gardin. After that they played only occasionally and then for relatively small stakes at games in which the skill and fun of beating your opponent is more important than the amount you win.

And bets, of course. They were constantly killing time by making bets on ridiculous and irrelevant things, usually five or ten dollar bets, but once in a while going higher when the thing they were betting on wasn't pure luck but was something on which they held divergent opinions. If they were alone in a bar, for instance, they'd sit in the middle and bet ten dollars on whether the next customer to enter it would go to the bar at the right or the left side of them. Whether the next customer to enter would be barefoot or wearing sandals—arguing over odds according to the weather and the time of day. If it had ever rained on Mars they would have bet on which raindrop of two would first reach the bottom of a pane. Ridiculous things, but the betting gave them something to talk about, for neither ever talked about himself, and talking about irrelevant things helped kill time.

Time was the enemy, although that was something neither of them talked about.

Once Crag took Gardin to his suite at the Luxor. Gardin had looked about him and whistled. "Where's the button you push for the dancing girls?" he wanted to know, and when Crag didn't answer, he asked, "You're a woman-hater, aren't you?" And when Crag didn't answer that, he let the subject drop.

Gardin wandered around the suite, hands in his pockets until he discovered the pornography room. Then he took his hands out of his pockets to look at the books and run a few of the tapes. Crag heard him chuckling to himself and saw a look on his face that disgusted him. "Come on out," he said. "Take some of those damn things home with you if you want, keep 'em, but don't read 'em here."

Gardin came out. His face was ugly now. "Pretty bluenose, aren't you?" he asked.

Crag shrugged. "What do you want to drink?"

"*Woji.* Unless you've got some *nephthin* around— wouldn't mind trying that once. No, I'm kidding."

Crag opened two *woji* bottles and handed one to Gardin with a glass.

Gardin poured himself a drink and put the bottle down by the chair he was sitting in. In a changed voice he said, "I'm feeling lousy, Crag. What's wrong with me?"

"You're getting soft."

"Soft?" Gardin stood up quickly. "Bet you a grand I can take you, here and now."

Crag grinned and for a moment something leaped inside him. Then he said, "No bet, Gardin. Sit down and drink your drink. I don't play Queensberry rules and you don't either. Once we got started if I didn't kill you you'd kill me. Let's not get into that, for a lousy grand bet or any other bet."

Gardin sat down but his face turned sullen. "Quit needling me then."

"I'm not needling you, just told you the truth. Hell, it's true about me too. I'm getting soft." But Crag didn't really believe it about himself.

Gardin was pacing around the suite again. He opened the double door that hid the six-by-eight video screen and whistled at the sight of it. "Boy, a big one. And that reminds me. Know what today is?"

"What?"

"Day they're going to land on Cragon. Been following the newscasts?"

"Not since yesterday. What gives?"

"The dust is gone. Didn't seem to settle, just to vanish all at once. And—this is impossible, but they say it's true—it's a finished planet."

Crag puffed a cigarette into flame. "What do you mean, a finished planet?"

"Not a raw one. Vegetation—trees and everything. Pretty much like Earth except it's mostly land instead of mostly ocean. But there are lakes and rivers—fresh water, and that doesn't make sense."

"Why doesn't it?"

"Streams and rivers get that way after rains, making channels for themselves over thousands of years of run-off from higher ground. Damn it, the planet's only two weeks old. How could the planet have formed river beds already?"

"Maybe it's precocious," Crag said.

"Whatever it is, it's not natural. Kid about it if you like, Crag, but even the toughest of the scientists are beginning to admit that this is something that couldn't happen naturally. Some of them are frank about saying they're scared stiff."

"Of what?"

"They don't know, and that's what scares them." Gardin turned back to the video screen. "I'd forgotten till I saw this, but it's about time for them to make a 'cast on that landing. Let's watch it. Okay?"

"Okay," Crag said. Gardin turned the switch and the

big screen leaped into color and sound, an almost naked Amazonian woman singing of the joys of a certain unmentionable perversion.

"Shut the damn thing off," Crag said.

"Okay, but it's only for a minute—" Gardin reached for the switch but before he could turn it the song ended and the picture faded.

And on the big screen flashed the distant picture of a planet seen from space. A planet that, except for the contour of the continents, could have been Earth. Blue oceans, continents mottled green and brown, white polar regions.

"We show you Cragon," said an unctuous voice, "newest planet of the sun. The view of it that you see is being 'cast from the flagship *Dorai*, and is from two hundred thousand miles out. We shall maintain this position until a report has been received from the scoutship *Andros*, which is even now proceeding down to make the first landing on the surface. In a few minutes—it will be at least another twenty before the *Andros* enters the atmosphere of Cragon—we will switch you to the scoutship so you can be *with* them at the very moment of landing. The scoutship is manned by Captain Burke and Lieutenant Laidlaw. We regret that the scoutship is too small to carry transspace video equipment so the view upon your screen will continue to be broadcast from here, from the flagship. But let us introduce you via tridi photos to the two men aboard the scoutship while we contact them for you by radio. Captain Burke."

A tridi still of a middle-aged man with hard eyes but a weak chin flashed on the screen. "Are you ready, Captain?" The lips of the photograph didn't move but a voice said, "Yes, Burke reporting, sir."

"Anything to report yet?"

"Only that we are descending slowly and cautiously, in accordance with instructions. We are a hundred miles up, still well above the outer reaches of the atmosphere."

"Good. Then there is time for you to introduce your companion. Please put Lieutenant Laidlaw on."

Another tridi still flashed on. A very handsome young

man with curly black hair. You would have expected his voice to be effeminate, and it was. "Lieutenant Laidlaw, sir."

"You are the one assigned to do the reporting while your captain navigates, Lieutenant. Am I right?"

"Yes, sir."

"Good. Then please remain at the microphone." The tridi photograph changed again to the distant view of a world revolving in space. "Have you chosen a point for your landing, Lieutenant?"

"Yes, sir. Approximately in the center of the day side, which is at the moment approximately in the center of the largest continent. Near the shore of a large lake—I think I can tell you which one. We have a monitor set here and are receiving your picture. Do you see a lake, almost exactly in the middle of your picture, that is roughly triangular in shape?"

"Yes, Lieutenant."

"Well, we plan on landing near the bottom point—the southern point of that triangle. You'll notice that a stream, or what looks like one, enters the lake at that point. And the area around the stream is green, but only a short distance from it is the edge of a large brown area. We figure that should be a good central point of observation. We can check the water of the stream and the water of the lake. And we can see what kind of vegetation makes up the green area and whether the brown area is sand or rock or what. Also our thermocouple observations indicate a temperature of about seventy degrees Fahrenheit, a nearly optimum temperature. We've got to land somewhere, and that looks like as good an all-around spot as any."

"Thank you, Lieutenant. And your altitude now?"

"A little under eighty miles. We're settling slowly, under antigrav."

Crag chuckled.

The Lieutenant's voice said, "Of course we'll make final observations before we make actual planetfall. We're now descending on automatics set to stop us at five miles. From there our telescopes will give us a very close view of the terrain. And by that time, we'll be within the atmosphere and can make a thorough check that will tell us whether it's breathable or whether we'll have to wear our suits."

"Thank you, Lieutenant Laidlaw. And now we will have a word from Admiral of the Grand Fleet Johnson, who is right here beside me aboard . . ."

Crag was chuckling again and Gardin turned away from the screen to look at him. "What's funny?" he wanted to know.

"The whole thing," Crag said. "They aren't going to land—or if they do they'll never take off again."

"Why not?"

"Not invited. Just watch."

Gardin grinned. "There's an old phrase—put your money where your mouth is. How much you want to bet?"

Crag shrugged. "You name it. But you'll lose."

Gardin was fumbling through bills. "Getting a little short, but I'll take a thousand of that. Or were you kidding?"

For answer Crag took a thousand-dollar bill out of his pocket and dropped it on the floor between them. Gardin covered it with ten hundreds.

The bulldog face of the admiral was on the screen. ". . . seems no danger whatsoever, but the fleet takes no chances. Before those men leave the scoutship, the area will have been surveyed for every possible danger. It seems impossible that a newly formed planet could possibly harbor life, inimical or otherwise, yet the possibility will not be overlooked. There are mysteries to which we do not have the answer—especially the mystery of how Cragon was formed and how it could so incredibly quickly have acquired atmosphere, a well-developed topography and, especially in so short a time, what is almost certainly vegetation. It is because of these mysteries that we shall not land a big ship and risk the lives of thousands.

"Captain Burke and Lieutenant Laidlaw have volunteered for this mission and know they are risking their lives, even though no risk *seems* apparent. But a new planet always is an unknown quantity and this applies doubly in the current case, when the details of its formation are so mysterious, so sudden that one might almost think it was the deliberate act of an intelligent entity.

"However, no difficulty is anticipated in making the landing. All factors are known there. The biggest question mark is the atmosphere. Will it be breathable as is, or will we have to set up atmosphere plants as we have on Mars and Venus and under the Callisto domes? Spectographic analysis—the only analysis we can make until we get there—is encouraging. Oxygen is present in approximately the same proportion as in the atmosphere of Earth; so is carbon dioxide. Atmospheric density is a little less than that of Earth, but only slightly so; Kaperhorn estimates that its density at sea level is approximately that of Earth's at an altitude of one mile, the altitude of, say, Albuquerque or Denver.

"The element of uncertainty lies in the fact that there are certain trace elements which we have been unable to analyze completely at a distance, and there is of course the possibility that one of these trace elements may be poisonous. The scoutship has no chemical laboratory aboard, but does have cages of canaries and other small experimental animals, the use of which will enable Captain Burke to decide whether, for a short period, it will be safe to leave the ship w'thout suits.

"But with or without suits they will explore the area immediately around their landing point—"

Crag made a rude noise. "Another *woji*, Gardin?"

Gardin nodded and Crag went to the bar, opened and brought back two fresh bottles. The sphere of the new planet was still on the screen but the voice of the Admiral had been supplanted by soft music. "What gives?" Crag asked. "Did he run out of crap to talk about?"

"Guess so. They're filling in until a report comes from the scoutship. Just a few minutes; it's nearing the top of the atmosphere now." Gardin glanced down at the money on the floor between them. "Crag, what was the crazy idea of making that ridiculous bet? You're practically giving me a grand."

"Maybe," Crag said.

"Unless you've got inside dope, and I don't see how you could have, but . . . you suggested the bet. I'm a sucker to bet a man at his own game."

Crag grinned at him. "Want to call it off? I'll give you a chance now, before the scoutship comes on."

Gardin hesitated a moment, then shook his head. "No, leave it lay." He took a long pull from his bottle.

The music stopped and the video spoke again with a human voice. "Lieutenant Laidlaw speaking from the scoutship. Captain Burke is at the controls. We are descending slowly, just entering the upper atmosphere of Cragon. That is, our instruments show a detectable pressure, although still not much above a laboratory vacuum. We are approximately fifty miles high and at the moment we are descending at the rate of five miles a minute, although we shall slow that rate of descent within a few minutes to avoid overheating the hull from atmospheric friction.

"Forty-five miles. We can see from here—I think with certainty—that the dark green areas of land of the surface really are forests. At least they give very much the same appearance as a dense Earth forest gives from the same height.

"We're thirty miles high now, almost into the stratosphere. But— Captain Burke is stopping our descent; we are holding position at this height, motionless. What's wrong, Captain?"

In the moment of silence Crag asked, "Want to double that bet?"

Gardin shook his head. "But how the hell—?"

"Never mind how the hell. Maybe I do have inside information. If you don't want to double it, I'll give you one last chance to call it off."

Gardin didn't hesitate. He scooped up the handful of bills, handed Crag his thousand and stuffed the ten hundreds into his own pocket. Crag grinned. "Now we'll see how he's going to work it."

"How who's going to work what?"

"Shhh," said Crag, as a different voice sounded from the video.

"Captain Burke taking the mike. And apologizing for the fact that the Lieutenant and I have been talking off mike for a moment. This is not an emergency, but something that must be investigated before we descend any lower. Something seems to be wrong with our air-conditioning system.

"At the point at which I stopped our descent I happened to glance at the cage in which we have three canaries—the use of which the Lieutenant explained to you a few minutes ago. And noticed that one of them is lying on the bottom of the cage and the other two seemed to be—well, in trouble.

"Obviously something has gone wrong with our air-conditioning system and we should not complete the descent until we have fixed it. The Lieutenant, who is more familiar than I with that part of the mechanism of the ship, is now investigating. I'll have his report—or give him back the microphone—in just a moment."

Just a moment passed. The Captain's voice spoke again. "Something strange here. Lieutenant Laidlaw reports that he can find nothing wrong with the equipment, that the indicators show proper proportion of oxygen and fail to indicate the presence of any foreign gas, and yet two of the canaries are now dead and the other apparently dying. The hamsters and the white rats are huddling together and breathing hard, showing signs of discomfort.

"And he and I seem to *smell*, very faintly, a foreign odor. I haven't checked with the lieutenant on this but I would classify it as something vaguely like sulphuric acid —but *sweetish*, as well. If you can imagine a mixture of sulphuric acid and gardenias—well, that's the way I'd describe it.

"Yet this ship is airtight—we are bringing in, even for

processing purposes, nothing of the atmosphere outside, tenuous as it is at a height of thirty miles. It must be something wrong right here in the ship itself. There is no way it can conceivably concern the planet we are near. There is no way—"

"Captain Burke!" It was the voice of the bulldog-faced admiral aboard the flagship. "Raise ship at once. Completely outside that atmosphere."

"Yes, Admiral."

"Keep reporting."

"Yes, Admiral . . . We're rising now. Thirty-three miles now, thirty-five. Lieutenant Laidlaw is staggering across the cabin toward me but he seems to be all right, maybe just off balance. And my headache—I didn't have time to mention it—is going away. Forty miles. I think we're out of it now, sir. Or our air-conditioning system is functioning properly again. Shall we try again, sir?"

"Report back to the fleet at once. Before we make another attempt, with a live or a drone ship, we want to check yours thoroughly. As well as your air-conditioning system, we want to check you and the Lieutenant, and those canaries."

"Yes, sir."

Gardin looked at Crag, and Crag laughed. He had, Crag realized, laughed more in the last half hour than he had for a long time.

"Bet you the drone ship doesn't land there either," Crag said.

"No bet." Gardin went over and shut off the video. "No use keeping on watching now. It'll be at least another day before they get a drone rigged up. Crag, what's it all about?"

Crag shook his head slowly. "Sorry. To tell you that I'd have to tell you too much about other things."

"It isn't something we can cash in on?"

Crag shook his head again. "Game of gin, to kill some time?"

Gardin stood up. "Sorry, I've got business. You might not be seeing me so much for a while, Crag. That thousand of mine you almost took—and thanks for calling off

the bet, since you must have known it was a sure thing—
was getting near rock bottom. I'm going to have to scrape
up some more."

"Good luck," Crag told him.

CHAPTER TEN

CRAG didn't see Gardin for longer than a week, although he continued to frequent the same places where he and Gardin had gone together. He didn't go to Gardin's hotel for two reasons; one, he knew that if Gardin was still there and wanted to see him, Gardin would do the looking up, and two, that Gardin might have left the hotel but left his woman there to wait for him. And he didn't want to see Gardin's brassy blonde without Gardin around. Preferably not even then.

He found himself following the newcasts about the new planet. None of them, after the fiasco of the would-be first landing, were telecast; they were merely reports. The space fleet couldn't hold back the facts, but they could avoid making fools of themselves by letting the public *watch* the failures.

No alien gas had been found in the hull of the scout-ship that had been recalled from the first attempt. The only concrete evidence found in it was the bodies of the two dead canaries and the fact that the third canary had been very ill. So had the hamsters, the mice and the two humans. The Captain and the Lieutenant had spent hours after their return recovering from nausea.

The air-conditioning equipment had been found to be functioning perfectly and autopsies on the dead canaries had given no indication whatsoever of the cause of death.

The only conclusion the investigating scientists could draw was that there must be a hitherto unknown ingredient in the atmosphere of Cragon, one so deadly that even in the rarefied atmosphere thirty miles above the surface it could penetrate the solid hull of a spaceship, possibly by some process akin to osmosis, and kill or injure the occupants. Space suits seemed to offer no answer; anything that can penetrate the foot-thick hull of a ship can certainly penetrate the airtight fabric of a space suit.

Two days after the initial failure at landing, a drone ship was sent down to land. Since the manned ship had brought back no sample of the deadly gas—only of its effects—it was assumed that it had leaked out again on the return trip across space and that the same thing would happen to any that the drone ship picked up, in whatever type container. So instead of containers, the drone was packed with chemical testing equipment, some of it automatic and some operable by remote control, that would make many and delicate tests *in situ*, while the drone rested on the surface of the planet, and record the results for later analysis.

The only trouble was that the drone ship never landed. Never, in fact, got into even the most tenuous upper reaches of the atmosphere. Cragon changed tactics. Well over two hundred miles above the surface of the planet the drone ship—*bounced.*

It had hit an impenetrable force field.

Not even unmanned rockets were welcome to land on Cragon.

Crag chuckled to himself.

That ended the official telecasts of the attempts to land on Cragon. The admiralty made a very carefully worded announcement to explain the news blackout that indicated that the admiralty was scared stiff.

"It now seems possible if not probable that the solar system has been invaded by a race of aliens. The formation of a new planet from the debris of the solar system was too strange and too sudden to be accounted for by any theory of astrophysics known to man; it is therefore considered possible that it was accomplished deliberately by an alien race from outside the system.

"That the intention of this race is not friendly is strongly indicated by the fact that they have refused peaceable contact, which could have been established had they let us land freely. A force field is not known in nature and must therefore be artificial. So must a poisonous gas which penetrates the solid hull of a ship, but which vanishes completely when that ship is outside the atmosphere.

"While the planet Cragon has, to our knowledge, committed no overt act against the rest of the solar system, and while therefore a state of war need not be assumed, a *state of emergency* must be declared. A state of *protective* emergency. Since it is possible that advance spies of the race of Cragonians are already among us, this will require henceforth a strict censorship of . . ."

The Solar Council immediately decreed a state of emergency, and doubled taxes on low incomes (and increased them slightly on high incomes) to finance whatever plans they were making. Which, of course, could not be made public because of the possibility of Cragonian spies.

But rumors were rife, especially in the spacemen's quarter, where rumors, especially concerning matters in space, were uncannily accurate. Although there was strict security on any reports from the asteroid belt that could have reached Marsfleet headquarters from the vicinity of Cragon, somehow the contents of those reports became known around the quarter almost within minutes of the time they could have been received. And known, Crag knew, correctly.

The second drone ship hadn't tried gentle descent on antigrav; it had blasted down at the surface with all rockets flaring; it had bounced off just the same—because of its tremendous speed crumpled into a single massive ingot of incandescent metal. Rockets with atomic warheads exploded on contact with the force field and subsequent telescopic-spectroscopic examination of the planet under the point of contact indicated that not even any of their radiation had penetrated that field to reach the atmosphere under it.

Cragon was off bounds.

And the spy scare grew. The military didn't know whether Cragon was populated or not or, if it was, what its inhabitants looked like—but the military was afraid and because it couldn't reach Cragon, it was looking for something it *could* reach, and that meant spies. Transients, other people who couldn't explain themselves readily, were picked up for questioning, and if their answers weren't ready and provable, they were questioned further, under drugs or otherwise.

The fact was something for Crag to think about; even though the rich who stayed at the luxury hotels were never bothered by the police—most of them, even if they were vacationing under aliases, were too powerful for the police to risk exposing—he realized that the military might overlook that obstacle. They might figure that a Cragonian spy would deliberately pose as a wealthy debauchee for that very reason. And the military were less susceptible to intimidation and bribery than the police, especially if they thought they might be dealing with an alien enemy spy.

So Crag took a precaution he hadn't bothered with before; he visited the best forger-printer in Mars and had papers made that gave him a complete false identity and history back to birth. They wouldn't stand up under a full-scale investigation, of course, but they'd cover him in case of any spot check or other casual inquiry.

Afterwards he wondered if he hadn't wasted the time and money, because they wouldn't protect him against any *serious* suspicion, and he'd already laid himself open to serious suspicion—if Gardin talked about him. He hadn't anticipated the spy-scare angle the day he and Gardin had watched the video of that first attempt at a landing on Cragon. He'd put himself in Gardin's hands by offering that bet of a thousand dollars at even odds that the scoutship wouldn't successfully land and take off again. How could he have known that, the military would want to know. Sure, he could tell them the truth —and admit to having killed Olliver, among other crimes.

Gardin himself might be suspicious, and if Gardin was, Crag couldn't blame him for reporting the incident. But Crag shrugged the thought off. After all, he had to take *some* chances. Did he want to live forever?

Which reminded him that he'd been taking too few chances to keep life interesting and that evening he let himself drink just a little more than usual in one of the toughest dives in the quarter and got into a fight. There's never difficulty in getting into a fight in the quarter.

He let himself be drawn into an argument, that was all, with four husky cargo handlers from the port. He didn't really know what he was arguing about but they didn't either. He let himself get argumentative about whatever it was and suddenly there was a fist coming at his face. He deflected it with his left hand and sank his right hand into the belly of the fist-thrower, who folded up like an accordion and started retching.

Crag stepped back from the bar and the other three of them came at him. He stepped under a haymaker and landed a light left to the solar plexus of the leading one, and then there were only two, but one of those two caught him a wallop on the side of the head that staggered him almost to the doorway. He came back, coming in low and using both fists like pistons and suddenly there was only one of them still interested. He was the biggest one, though, and Crag made him last a little longer by using only his right.

It had all happened so suddenly that Crag was scarcely breathing hard, although his ears rang from the one hard blow he'd taken. He walked back to the bar·to pick up his drink again. The bartender, a sizable club clenched tightly in his hand and his face a bit pale, backed away.

Crag nodded at him reassuringly. "It's okay," he said. "Nobody hurt, no damage done. And you don't have to join the party unless you want to."

The bartender relaxed. Crag took the final gulp of his drink and put a bill on the bar. "Give 'em each a drink on me when they come around," he said. And left.

It had been fun while it lasted, but—

He wondered where Gardin was, what kind of a job he was casing or doing. He wondered whether if he, Crag, had been getting low on funds too, Gardin would have asked him in the deal. And whether he'd have accepted, if Gardin had. He *thought* he'd trust Gardin enough, but . . .

But he was a long way from being near enough broke to give him excuse to plan another job. He still had well over nine-tenths of that damned half million. Half a million dollars was a lot of money, too much money. Damn money.

Or, more accurately, he thought, damn a man who couldn't find pleasure in the spending of it.

Back in his suite, too early, he opened the doors of the big video screen and flicked it on. Not because, if there was any new news about the new planet, he'd get it here, but he was curious about what kind of a stall the government was giving the people; they'd *have* to allow the newscasters to feed the public something, whether true or not.

But the screen flashed into the picture of a handsome gray-haired commercial announcer. His smile was so disgustingly sincere that Crag waited to see what he was going to say. And stepped closer to the screen because he knew what was going to happen when he heard it.

"Are you a *necrophile?* All your problems are solved. General Plastics now brings on the market a *similacrum* that is almost completely indetectable, except for the fact that it does not deteriorate, from a real dead body. Available in models of either sex, it sells for a low, low price. Or can be rented if, like most nonfetishist necrophiles, you prefer a change from time to time in the object of—"

Crag kicked in the screen.

Seven hundred dollars, he'd learned by now, was the cost of replacement of a screen on that video. And his suite cost two thirty and he'd managed to spend about a hundred otherwise. Another day, another thousand dollars. But even at that rate, half a million was going to last a long time. What was Gardin doing?

He went out on the balcony and stared up at the sky. The new planet wasn't in sight; it was still below the horizon. Anyway, to hell with it.

Earth was in the sky, though, and he stared at it for a while, wondering if he should go back there for a while. But why? Earth was just as corrupt, just as decadent as Mars. Neither had anything to offer that the other hadn't, except that Earth was more crowded.

And just a bit better policed, which made it just a bit less dangerous than Mars.

He went back in and to the bar and got himself a drink. Was that the only answer, drink, escape? Hell, if he had nothing better to do than to escape, why didn't he kill himself and get it over with? Why, except that a tiger doesn't commit suicide, even with *nephthin*, which lets him take however-many along with him in the process.

He drank enough to make him slightly sleepy, although he didn't feel it otherwise, and went to bed.

And slept, and dreamed. About a bronze-haired beautiful woman who was his wife—and in the dream, he didn't know that she had betrayed and deserted him, because it hadn't happened yet, and he was crazy in love with her. Only gradually—and yet understandably, because in dreams things that don't make sense otherwise are understandable—she changed. Her hair stayed the same, but she became more beautiful, more and more loved—and farther and farther away from him at the same time, and across a void of space and time he was calling out to her "Judeth! Judeth!" And wasn't aware of the change, didn't know that that hadn't been his wife's name. Because in that dream all women were the woman; there was only one woman and had never been any others. And then she came to him and he put his arms around her and—in the sudden quick inconsequence of dreams he was holding in his arms a dead woman, a corpse, and then his arms were empty as the corpse disintegrated and—

The phone was buzzing.

He swung himself to the edge of the bed and picked it up. "Yes?"

"Ah—Mr. Ah. There is a telephone call for you. A woman who refuses to give her name. But she says it is very important, a matter of life and death. Shall I—?"

"Put her on." He didn't ask for privacy on the circuit, although he had a hunch who it might be and what it might be about; because asking for a closed circuit was sure to make the management curious enough to listen in, whereas otherwise they wouldn't bother. In Mars City, only one woman could be calling him here.

"Yes?" he said.

It was the voice he expected, Bea's. It said, "I don't want to give my name, but you'll know who I am when I tell you we met at—"

"I know who you are," he interrupted. "What's the matter?" Although he could guess that, too.

"Our—mutual friend. I won't mention his name, but if you recognize my voice, you know who I mean. He's in an awful jam; I don't think there's anything you can do, but—"

"Where are you? Try to tell me without naming it."

"At our apartment. But I don't think it's going to be safe here. I'd better get out right away. Can you meet me at—at the place where he and you once played *mara* with three spacemen just back from a Callisto run and they tried to work a squeeze play on you in the game and you—"

"I'll be there in ten minutes," Crag said, and put down the phone.

He threw on clothes and dashed cold water into his face. He felt—awake, with danger and action impending.

CHAPTER ELEVEN

IT WAS a bar like any bar, except for the few swanky expensive ones in the quarter. Crag made it in ten minutes, but Bea was there before him. Had apparently just got there, for she was just sliding into a booth at the side. A big cargo walloper from the Port had seen her come in and was just swaggering over from the bar to open negotiations, whatever type of negotiations he had in mind. Crag would have liked a fight, but there wasn't the time for one, so he walked fast and got there ahead of the dock hand, spoke to Bea by name—not her right one of course—and slipped into the booth across from her. The dock hand stood a moment, irresolute, and then went back to where he'd been standing at the bar.

Crag's first question was, "Do minutes, or seconds matter?"

She leaned forward and he could see that she'd been crying, although she'd covered the signs with make-up and they wouldn't show at a distance of more than a couple of feet. "I don't think so," she said. "But I don't know what you can *do,* if anything, but he's—"

"Wait, then." Crag got out coins and pushed several into the slot of the musicon at the end of the booth, turned up the volume control. The place was too quiet, and their conversation might have carried. A voice blared at them. "I'd like to get you on a slow ship to Venus! Honey-wunny-bunny—"

Crag winced, but didn't turn down the volume. He leaned close and said, "All right, give it to me fast."

"It was a jewel job, wholesale place. Curme's, on the top floor of the Rasher building, about ten blocks north of—"

"I know where it is. Go on."

"He's caught in there, and they've got a cordon around

142

the place, around the whole block, and helis over the roof. He must have tripped an alarm or—"

"Is he alone?"

"Yes, he was working solo. He's been casing the place for two weeks and—"

"No one knew about it—except you?"

"Right. It must have been an alarm circuit. There's *no* way they could have been tipped off. It's not a cross. It's—"

"How do you know about it? I mean, about the fact that he's trapped now?"

She opened her purse and took out what looked like a fairly large make-up compact. She said, "It's a two-way; he carries the other end of it, except his looks like a tobacco pouch, and—"

"I've seen it. He called you on it, from Curme's?"

"Yes. It makes a faint buzz when he calls. And when he's on a job, I keep it right close in case he calls and there's anything I can do or—"

"What did he ask you to do? Notify me?"

"No, this time he didn't want anything—except to say so-long to me. He said it was hopeless, that they had every exit blocked solid—there are dozens of cops, hundreds maybe—and all he wanted me to do was get out of the apartment quick, before they got there to get *me*. I stayed long enough to call you, and then I got."

"They know who he is?"

She nodded. "I don't know how—unless one of them got a look at him when he was firing out a window and recognized him, but the loud-speaker they set up is calling him by name to come out and give himself up. That's how he knew they'd find out where he lived and get there to the apartment and why he called me to warn me to—"

"Can you call him back on that thing now?"

"Yes, but—"

"Get him, fast. Tell him I want to talk to him, and then put me on."

She held up the compact and opened it; there was a mirror inside the top and she pretended to be looking into it, and, after pressing a button somewhere, pretended to be talking to Crag.

"Gardin? You know who this is. And a friend of yours is here and wants to talk to you—you'll know his voice."

Crag reached for the tiny two-way; he held it as though he was examining it. And he talked as though he was talking to the woman across from him. "Let's talk fast, Gardin, before they might get a tracer beam on this thing and get to us here. They know where and who you are, so don't be coy on that end. What's the score?"

"They've got me bottled." The tiny, tinny voice just reached his ear over the blare of the music. "Nothing you can do about it, but thanks. They've got over a hundred cops here."

"How long can you hold out?"

"As long as I want to. They're not coming in to shoot it out. They'll wait till I give up or get bored and go through the door to shoot it out with them."

"How long can you hold out, damn it? In days or hours."

"Hell, a week if I have to. There's no food here but I won't starve in less than that. And there's plenty of water."

"Ammunition?"

"Whole rack of guards' weapons besides the one I brought. They know I'm well heeled."

"Can they gas you out?"

"Not without firing gas shells through the windows, and they're not going to take a chance on that. Why should they? They've got me cold, and they *like* sieges."

"Okay, hold out, Gardin, I'll get you out of there. May be a few days, but I'll get you."

"You can't. Don't try. It's—"

"I'm not telling you how in case they're finding this beam. Or exactly when, even if I knew. But hold out, damn it, and I'll get you out of there."

Crag snapped shut the compact and stood up quickly. "Come on, we're getting out of here, in case the cops did get on that beam and are tracing it now."

There was a helicab waiting outside and he pushed

Bea into it and followed her in, gave the address of another bar. Once Bea grabbed his arm. "Crag, it's suicide
—you *can't*—"

He shook off her grip. "We can, if he can hold out two
days. Maybe we can do it in less, if we can get some
more manpower. Has Gardin any other friends you'd
trust in this?"

"One, Crag. Hauser. But—the cops are looking for him
already He's in hiding and that's why you haven't met
him And it's a rough rap; he's—"

"Good. That makes him just the one we want, he's got
nothing to lose. You can reach him?"

"Of course, but—"

"Don't argue. We'll go in the bar I told this cabby to
take us to, so it doesn't look funny to him; we're almost
there anyway. One quick drink; then split up and here's
what you do. Stay away from Gardin's apartment—he's
probably right that they're there by now. Get Hauser,
come with him to the Luxor, if he'll come. Or—do you
want to go through with this, Bea? I can get Gardin
alone, but it'll take longer."

They were entering the bar and Crag ordered quickly,
then turned to Bea. "Well," he said, "made your mind
up?"

"It's been made up all along. You're going right to the
Luxor?"

"I've got a few things to buy first. How long will it
take you to get this Hauser, or find out that you can't
get him?"

"At least two hours. Unless I risk phoning him, and
since he's in hiding he asked me not to."

"Don't phone him then. But I'll get to the Luxor before you do, in that case. Good luck, Bea."

They downed their drinks and Crag left first. He
headed straight for an aircar agency and bought himself
a six-place Dragoon, paid cash, and a premium price, to
get the demonstrator model that was already on the roof,
gassed and ready to go. He landed it on the roof of the
Luxor only minutes later.

The attendant ran to get it and to put it away. Crag

asked him, "Is there a store near that sells tools, hardware?"

"Yes, sir, about three blocks north on—"

"Can you go there right away and buy me three shovels and put them in the car?"

"Right now, sir, I'm afraid I couldn't take off for that long. Perhaps one of the bellboys—"

Crag handed him a hundred-dollar bill. "I don't want to waste time. You send one of the bellboys, fast. Large sand shovels And split the change out of this between you. Also don't bury that aircar behind any others. Keep it out where I can take off the second I come back on the roof."

"Yes, sir." Since the shovels wouldn't cost over ten dollars apiece, it was a generous enough tip to get fast service on both them and on the aircar.

Crag took the elevator down to his suite and let himself in. He buzzed the desk. "Two people are coming to see me. Send them up without delay the minute they get here."

"Yes, sir. Their names?"

"Never mind what names they give. Send up anyone who asks for me "

He tossed a few things into a small suitcase. To hell with the rest of it; he wouldn't need it where he was going.

He took a screwdriver and unscrewed the plate of the main fluorescent switch, the first of the four hiding places in each of which he had stashed a hundred thousand dollars.

The money wasn't there. Crag swore and was beginning to work on the second of the hiding places—whoever had searched his room couldn't possibly have found *all* of them—when the door buzzer sounded and he went to answer it.

Bea stood there, and there were two other people with her. A small man, shifty-eyed and bald, but tough-looking, and a small dark Gypsy-looking woman—beautiful except for her eyes; they were the small beady eyes of a rodent.

Crag let them in and locked the door behind them.

"Crag, this is Hauser, and Gert. He says he'll help us get Gardin, but his woman has to go along—especially if we're all heading anywhere afterward."

Crag nodded. "Okay. Go in the bar and make drinks. We're almost ready; I've got one thing to do."

There was no money in the second cache. Or in the third or the fourth.

He went into the bar. "Job for you," he said. "Put down the drinks. I had money, big money, hidden in four different places in this suite. It's gone, from all of them. That means somebody watched me doing the hiding. No kind of a search—not even a squad of cops spending weeks at it—would have found all four of those places. That means there are one-way observation panels looking into this suite. Help me find them."

Hauser said, "Probably the mirrors. You've got them all over and they're set into the wall, not hanging. I worked a luxury hotel once and that's the usual thing, the mirrors."

Crag nodded. There was a mirror in the wall beside where he was standing, a small one. He picked up a bottle and smashed at the mirror; it crashed through, showing space, a passageway, behind it. But the space was too small for him to get through and he picked up another bottle and went out into the living room, looking for a big mirror. He found one and smashed it out.

Hauser was behind him. "Going to get your money back? Want help? I've got a heater."

Crag stepped through the space where the mirror had been. "This is a private deal; I'll take care of it. Keep the women amused but see that nobody drinks too much. We're going to have work to do."

There was a maze of passageways; every room of his own suite and of all the other suites on the floor were under observation from at least one mirror. Especially the bedrooms. And the passageways were used; there wasn't a bit of dust on their floors. Probably, besides their uses for criminal purposes, these passageways were rented occasionally to favored patrons, voyeurs, those who would rather watch than do. Well, the voyeurs would have been disappointed in watching the doings in Crag's suite.

Not so the suite adjacent. As he passed its master bedroom he couldn't help seeing through a big mirror that the three women who had welcomed him on his own arrival, the blonde, the brunette and the redhead, had all three been kept by the renter of the adjacent suite. And were very busy, all three of them.

He had to pass a lot of mirrors, a lot of suites, before he found steps leading downward. And from what he couldn't help seeing, he decided that he liked the clientele of the Luxor even less than he liked its management. There may have been those among the clientele who went in for ordinary unperverted sexual amusements, but he didn't happen to see any of them.

However, he wasn't interested in censoring morals, but in getting his money back. And he had a strong hunch, almost a certainty, that the management was responsible for the theft. He remembered now the gleam behind Carleton's pince-nez glasses when he had pulled out a sheaf of big bills to make an advance payment on the suite. Probably the manager had from that moment posted a bellboy or other menial to watch and see whether Crag would cache money in his quarters. The bellboy would have been in on it, of course, but he'd have been lucky if the manager had given him a single thousand out of the four hundred thousand.

He didn't investigate what was going on in any of the other floors of suites—one had been more than enough. He counted flights of stairs down until he knew he was on the main floor. And there he started looking for, and found, a panel that was locked from the other side. That would be either the manager's private office or his personal quarters. There was no peephole or one-way mirror here, of course, so he didn't know what was on the other side and picked the lock as silently as he had ever picked one in his life.

He inched open the panel quietly. It opened into the manager's office, and he could see Carleton's back only a yard from him. The manager was seated at an ornate desk, leafing through a sheaf of papers.

Crag stepped through and closed the panel behind him. He reached his right hand around the scrawny neck of the manager, squeezing just hard enough to prevent any outcry and pulling back just far enough to keep Carleton's frantically groping hands from reaching any of the buttons on or under the desk.

He said quietly. "If you don't already guess, or recognize my voice, you'll know who this is when I tell you I want four hundred thousand dollars. Where is it?"

He relaxed pressure enough to permit a whisper, and when none came he tightened his fingers again.

A trembling hand came up and pointed to a metal door with a combination knob set in the wall directly across the office. Crag relaxed pressure enough to hear a croaking voice: "Left four, then six, one, eight."

Crag pulled him out of the chair, to his feet. "Come on. You're going with me while I open it. If there's an alarm and any help comes, you'll die the second it gets here." He walked the man across the room until they stood facing the safe, Carleton between Crag and the knob. He reached, with his free left hand, around Carleton's body.

Carleton squeaked, but it sounded like, "Don't!" and Crag grinned and relaxed pressure on his throat a little. "Trap?"

"Yes. It's booby-trapped. We'll both die if we're standing here. I'll open it. Let me open it."

Crag let him open it. Besides ledgers and tapes there were two money boxes in the vault. "Which?" Crag asked. The strangling manager pointed weakly at one of them. "That one. It's mine. The other's hotel money."

Crag held onto the neck. "Pick them both up. Carry them to your desk and open them there."

He waited until the second box was opened and the lid thrown back. Then gently, very gently, he tapped the manager behind the ear with his metal left hand. It would have given Crag pleasure to strike harder, but it was not in his nature to kill unnecessarily. He lowered

Carleton into his chair, ripped off part of his clothing and bound and gagged him securely with it.

He took the large denomination bills out of both boxes; he didn't count them but obviously there was considerably more than the four hundred thousand dollars which had been his. He went back through the panel, closing and locking it behind him, and back up the stairs, counting flights again.

The three people he'd left in his suite—Bea, Gert and Hauser—had followed him through the broken mirror and were standing watching events through one of the one-way panels, the one where the blonde-brunette-redhead trio were operating. "Come on," he told them. "We've got to get out of here fast."

They didn't argue. They followed him back into the suite, out into the corridor and up to the roof via the elevator.

"Shovels?" he asked the attendant.

"In the aircar, sir. And—"

"Thanks, I see where it is." He ran toward it, the others following. He got in and made a fast takeoff.

"What did you mean asking him about shovels?" Bea asked him. He saw she'd brought an open bottle with her, and took it firmly from her and threw it out the window of the aircar. He said, "No more drinking till we're through. We've got work to do—if you want me to get Gardin out of there."

"But—shovels! You can't *dig* him out of the top floor of a twenty-story building."

Crag didn't answer. He was getting every mile of speed possible out of the aircar, heading south of the city. He didn't speak again, even to answer questions, until they were an hour away. Then he told Bea, "Get Gardin on that two-way of yours. Tell him we can make it in a few hours, if he can hold out that long."

"But we're heading away from Mars City, Crag. How can—?"

"Never mind. Do what I told you."

Bea took out the box, talked into it briefly, and listened. "He's doing fine, says he can hold out as long as he has to. But he can't believe there's any way you can get him out of there. He says there are at least two hundred cops, and six helis overhead. They can shoot down any-thing—"

"Tell him not to worry, just to hold out."

She talked briefly again and then closed the box. She turned in the seat to face Crag. "All right," she said, "I told him. But why can't you tell us and him what you're going to try? We're all in this."

"All right," he said. "I've got a spaceship hidden. We're going to get it. We rescue him in it. I can put it so he can step right from the window into the port."

"My God, a *spaceship* right down in Mars City. That's —" She laughed suddenly. "I started to say that's illegal, but—" She hesitated. "It might work, Crag. But why can't I tell Gardin? It'll make him feel better if he knows you're going to try something that's got a chance of working?"

"It's got better than a chance of working. But the cops may have tapped that beam by now and be monitor-ing it. Then they'd be ready for us and it wouldn't work. Nothing those helis can throw can touch a spaceship, nor anything they've got there for the siege, on the ground or in the building. But if they knew in advance, they could have a bigger spaceship waiting for us. Or an atomic cannon or two ready to shoot us down."

"But they'll *get* ships from the spaceport, Crag."

"And we'll be to hell and gone off Mars by the time they get one off the ground. Now shut up. I'm hedge-hopping this aircar and that takes concentration at night."

Two hours later he put it down. He pointed in the dim light of Phobos and Demos to a dune of sand ahead. "The ship's in that," he said. "Hauser, bring those shovels out of the back and—"

"Shovels?" There was horror in Hauser's voice. "It'll take us months to shovel all that sand. Why don't we go and get a sand-cat?"

"That's the way I buried it. But it'll take hours to get one and drive it here. And we don't have to uncover the ship, damn it; all we have to do is to get a trench through to the port, and it's dead center on this side. Once I get in the ship I can rock it on the antigravs and most of that sand will roll off by itself and we can lift out of what's left."

They started shoveling. Crag worked continuously and made Hauser do the same, although after a while Hauser had to stop and rest on his shovel once in a while. The two women took turns with the third shovel; Crag hadn't known when he'd bought only three that there'd be a fourth in the party.

Hauser was panting. "My God, Crag," he said. "This is still going to take hours. Didn't you bring any grub? I'm getting hungry."

"Dig faster then," Crag told him. "There's food in the ship. Can you pilot one of these things?"

Hauser wiped sweat from his forehead and then shook his head. "Gardin can, though. Where we going in it? Venus?"

"We'll decide that when we get Gardin."

Even with three of them shoveling at a time, it was a longer and harder job than Crag had estimated it to be. It was dawn when they finally uncovered the port of the spaceship and got it open. Bea had wanted several times to call Gardin on the two-way, but Crag had forbidden it, since if the police had found the beam and were monitoring it, they could trace it directionally and the spaceship would never get off the ground.

Once in the ship, it was a tougher job than Crag had realized to use the antigravs to get rid of the rest of the sand. At first it seemed too solidly embedded for him to rock even a fraction of an inch. But finally he could rock it an inch, and then inches, and at last it was free, and rose.

He hedge-hopped it back to Mars City and because he couldn't use full speed at so low an altitude, it took almost an hour. En route Hauser and the two women gorged themselves with food from the ship's food locker —but drank nothing because Crag had taken the key from the locker that contained bottled goods and told them that no one would have another drink until they were safely away with Gardin—and then, exhausted from the digging, they slept.

Crag called out from the control panel and woke them when he was only a few minutes away from Mars City. He told Bea to get Gardin on the two-way and tell him to be ready near the center on the north side of the building.

It went like clockwork. Due to Crag's skill in jockeying the ship into exact position, the actual rescue was so easy that after their long labor in getting and freeing the ship, it was almost anticlimactic. From the ground, from windows and roofs of other buildings and from helicopters hovering overhead the police poured fire at them from every available weapon. But the fire which would have melted an air car within seconds barely warmed the thick and insulated hull of a spaceship. And the instant Gardin was inside and the port had closed, Crag flashed the ship upward, set a course and locked the controls.

"Safe now," he said. "They'll have ships after us within minutes, but they won't catch us."

"Are you sure?"

"Yes. We can't fight back because this baby doesn't carry armaments, but because of that it's faster than anything that does."

"But where are we going?" Gardin asked. "They'll have tracers on us; we can't land on Mars without their knowing where. Venus?"

"Cragon," Crag said.

"Cragon! Nothing can land on Cragon. Not even the whole space fleet."

Crag grinned at him. "That's why we'll be safe there."

CHAPTER TWELVE

THERE was argument, even after he had explained. But all of them and especially the two women, at first thought Venus was a better idea.

A new, raw planet, they argued, wasn't civilization. On Venus they'd all be rich. Gardin had brought a bag of fabulous jewels with him from the rescue; he'd had plenty of time while under siege to pick them out. Their value was anybody's guess, but it couldn't be less than a million dollars, even sold through a fence; and Gardin was willing to split with the rest of them for having rescued him.

Of course there'd be a risk to landing on Venus; they'd have to land in a remote spot and hide the spaceship, as Crag had done on Mars. But once they got into a city and cashed in some of the jewels, they'd be safe enough. Even if identified, they'd be rich enough to buy immunity from extradition and still have plenty left.

"What good will jewels be on Cragon?" Bea wanted to know.

"You can wear them," Crag told her. "You'll be the best dressed women on the whole planet."

But Crag won, gradually talked them over. Gardin came to his side first, then Hauser; finally the women assented.

Two days later they approached Cragon. Crag took over the controls. Because the others wanted him to, remembering what had happened to the atmosphere inside the scoutship which had made the first landing attempt, Crag lowered very slowly, ready to raise ship fast if any of them started to experience difficulty in breathing. But none of them had, so he set the ship down in a gentle, perfect landing.

Just as the ship touched surface a voice in Crag's mind said, "Welcome, Crag." He answered mentally, not aloud, and looked quickly at the others to see if they had received any equivalent message; obviously none of them had.

Crag opened the port without bothering to check the atmosphere outside. He knew it would be good Earth-type air, and it was. It had a clear, cool sweetness that made the breathing of it almost a caress for the lungs. The others stepped down after him.

"Well, we're here," Gardin said. "Now what?"

"A drink," Bea suggested. "A lot of drinks."

Crag hesitated, then handed her the key to the locker. "All right," he said. "Break it out and we'll celebrate."

Bea went inside the ship and came out again shortly with an open *woji* bottle. She looked disgusted. "Big deal, that liquor supply," she said. "Ten bottles, two apiece. What are we going to do when they're gone?"

"Do without," Crag said. "Or find some equivalent of wild grapes and learn how to make our own."

"Damn it, Crag," Bea said. "If you knew when we were leaving Mars, why didn't you stock up the ship? After we picked up Gardin we could have raided some outpost station and—well, at least have stocked up on *liquor*, enough to last us a while."

Crag shrugged. Actually he'd thought of doing just that and had decided not to; the ship couldn't have carried enough liquor to have lasted five of them for their lifetimes anyway and so the sooner they learned to do without or to make their own the better.

He took the bottle when it was passed to him but took only a sip from it. He was more interested right now in looking around him and planning. He'd brought the ship down near a clear, gently meandering stream. He had no doubt that it was clean sweet water. A grassy plain sloped down to it. Beyond the stream was forest; some of the trees looked familiar to him, others strange. But no doubt they'd find edible things, good things. Everything they needed. Meat? As though in answer to his unspoken question—although he knew the alien who had made all this wasn't invading his privacy by listening in his mind —he heard the far cry of an animal of some kind. And in the stream a fish leaped. Yes, everything they needed.

And probably dangers, too. He'd bet odds that there were predators there, hunters as well as hunted. Well, that was to the good. Nothing that is easy is fun; he'd learned that lesson at the Luxor.

A bottle was being handed to him and he saw that it was a fresh one. Again he took a sip, but as he passed it on he held out his hand toward Bea. "The key," he said. "That'll be enough for now. We've got work to do."

"Work? Already? We just got here. You mean you're not going to let us hang one on, to celebrate?"

Crag hesitated, and then shrugged. Why not? He'd landed on the day side but near the twilight zone; it would soon be evening. Why not let them hang one on, and himself with them; in the morning would be time to start planning and working. Besides, the five of them, all heavy drinkers, would probably kill the ten bottles and that would end the problem of liquor rationing. Why not get rid of it all at once?

"All right," he said. "We'll have a party. But first let's gather a lot of wood for a fire. It's cramped for us in the spaceship; we've had enough of that for a while."

"But why a fire?" Hauser wanted to know. "It's not cool."

"Probably will be after dark and it'll be too late to get wood then. Besides—" Crag gestured toward the forest across the stream. "—we don't know what might come out of those woods after dark. If something does come out, we want to be able to see it."

Hauser frowned. "What makes you think there might be anything dangerous, Crag? According to you, this—alien made this world to please you. Why'd he put anything in it that could hurt you?"

Crag said grimly, "Because he knows me and *did* make it to be the way I'd want it to be. Which would not be all lambs and no lions. Would you want it that way, Gardin?"

Gardin grinned. "Maybe not, but neither would I want it all water and no *woji*. Well, we haven't looked very far yet. Maybe there are streams that run *woji*. All right, gang, let's gather sticks."

Sticks were easy to find, just across the stream. Crag stationed Hauser to mount guard with a heatgun while the other four did the gathering; within an hour, just about as the sun was going down, they had an ample supply to keep a fair-sized fire burning through the night, in case they spent the whole night in the open.

And within another hour they admitted it had been a wise precaution—at least as far as warmth was concerned; otherwise the cool evening would have forced them back into the crowded quarters of the ship. Thy drank a bit, then brought out food from the ship and ate, then started in on their celebration, heavy drinking.

All but Crag, that is. For a while he took drink for drink with the others and then found himself taking more and more time between drinks, and not minding it. He told himself that one of them—and it might as well be he—should stay nearly enough sober to be sure the fire was kept going, and to be able to guard the others. But there was also the fact that he found himself wanting each drink less than the preceding one.

He'd never especially liked the taste of liquor; he'd drunk for effect, escape. And here. . . .

By midnight—and Cragon had a period of rotation, of night and day, almost exactly the same as Earth's—all the liquor was gone and the others were drunk. And it was getting quite cold by then and Crag helped them help one another back into the ship and into bunks.

Then he went back outside, replenished the fire and sat in front of it. Alone. He didn't dare sleep, so he didn't. He could have, of course, in the ship, with the port shut, but he didn't want to have to go back in there, even for a few hours. It was better to be out here, alone, even if he had to stay awake. He could stay awake for days on end if he had to; and he often had.

In the morning—after the most beautiful sunrise he had ever seen—he was a little tired. But felt better than the others looked as though they felt, when he'd routed them out. Gardin admitted to a bad hangover, but didn't show it. The others admitted to hangovers and showed them. They were moody over breakfast.

"Well, *Boss*," Bea asked, "what are our orders for today? Or are we going to vote on what to do? Is this a democracy, or are you running it?"

"We'll vote if you want," Crag said. "But vote or no vote, there are certain things we've got to do ahead of other things. We need living quarters. That ship's too crowded and has too little privacy for five people to live in long. It's crowded, even for four. We've got to start on some adobe huts—small ones will do at first; we can build decent ones later."

"What's adobe?" Hauser wanted to know.

"Clay shaped into bricks and left to dry in the sun. If we scout both ways along that creek we'll find some clay."

"Mud huts? We're going to live in *mud huts?*" Gert sounded horrified.

Crag looked at her. "If you've got any better ideas—outside of five people trying to live in that ship—let's have them. And there's the question of food. I'd guess there's enough in the ship for five of us for another few days, a week if we go on rations. But we've got to learn how to hunt and fish, and start that right away. Gardin, you're a good shot, aren't you?"

Gardin nodded.

"Then here's my suggestion for today. Try that forest and see what you can find. Go heavily armed and don't go in too deep, because we don't know what we'll run into there. We want to learn the dangers gradually, not by one of us getting killed the first day. If you want me to go with you I will, but—"

Gardin said, "I won't need help. But what do you have in mind for yourself?"

"To scout along the stream for some clay. I once knew a little geology, not much, but I can probably recognize the kind of stuff we need better than any of the rest of you. If I find a deposit near, okay. If I find one but too far to carry bricks, we'll move headquarters, move the spaceship nearer to it. Hauser, have you ever done any fishing?"

"No."

"Good, then you won't have any preconceptions about it, and it'll probably be different here from on Earth anyway. Find some wire and make hooks, try to find out what bait they'll take. Or figure a way of making nets. Or make yourself a fish spear and try it out; the water's clear and there are places where it's shallow enough. Or —hell, just figure us a way of getting some fish, that's all. Okay?"

Hauser nodded, not too happily.

"And us?" Bea asked. I suppose you've got *our* day planned too."

"I'd suggest you gather firewood for a starter, plenty of it. After that, we'll see. If I find a clay deposit you can help me get a start on making adobe bricks. Or if Gardin gets game, you can try your hand at skinning it—if it's got fur—and cooking it. Or see what you can figure out in the way of net making to help Hauser." He grinned. "Don't worry; there'll be plenty for you to do."

"I'm not worrying," Bea said. "Not about *that*." She glared at him.

Crag said, "I'm not a boss here. Those weren't orders, but they're all things that have to be done if we're going to survive. Anybody want to trade assignments, or add any other suggestions?"

"Yes," Gert said. "This is a hell of a place to have brought us. We should have gone to Venus."

"Maybe we should have," Gardin said. "But it's too late now. There isn't enough fuel in the ship even to get us back to Mars. We made our choice when we took off from Mars—and you can blame Crag if you want for talking us into this, but that isn't going to change things. Let's get going."

They got going. Crag had first luck; he found an excellent clay deposit only fifty yards upstream. He made a few bricks and put them in the sun to see how long they'd take to dry, and then came back. Bea and Gert had gathered some firewood and were moodily watching—not helping—Hauser file a barb on wire he'd bent into the approximate shape of a fishhook.

Clay told them about the clay and suggested they come and help him make more bricks.

Bea glared at him defiantly. "We talked that over, Crag. *We* don't want other quarters—not mud huts, anyhow. We're willing to sleep in the ship. You're the one who wants a private house and why should we help you?"

Crag sighed but decided not to argue. If the women were going to be recalcitrant, it was up to their men to put them into line and he wasn't going to mix in their domestic problems. Sooner or later they'd get tired of the spaceship bunks and change their minds. And when the food supply of the ship ran out they'd be in much better mood to help with other tasks.

He went back to his clay deposit and his brick making.

Hauser caught no fish that day. Gardin came back in late afternoon carrying one small rabbit-like animal. He seemed discouraged. "Saw several of these but wasted most of my shots. My God, but the things are fast."

He said he'd seen one bigger animal but at too great a distance to make a good guess at what type it was, and he couldn't stalk it closely enough to get in a shot at it. "Guess I'm a better city hunter than a country one," he admitted. "I can follow a man across a city for days and never lose him, but wild animals—guess it's out of my line. How'd the rest of you do?"

Just looks answered him, from Hauser and the two women.

Crag shook his head slowly. "Gardin, I guess I made a mistake. If you don't like it here, if this isn't a life for you, I guessed wrong. Do you still want to go to Venus and take your chances there?"

"Want to? Crag—maybe I could adjust here if Bea could, but all I have to do is to look at her to get the answer to that. Yes, we want to go to Venus. I'll swap a million dollars worth of jewels for enough fuel to get us there."

"Keep the jewels," Craig said. "The tank isn't almost

empty; there's enough in it to get you to Venus. I jimmied the gauge on the way here, once while the rest of you were sleeping. I wanted to give Cragon a chance; I wanted you to land here *thinking* you were here for keeps. Take the ship and get going."

Both the women had leaped to their feet. Hauser was grinning.

Crag nodded. "Take it. Just unload whatever supplies you won't need on the trip. And whatever tools, and all the weapons and ammunition except a sidearm apiece for you and Hauser. And take this." He handed Gardin a thick roll of bills, the money he'd taken from the two boxes that had been in the Luxor safe.

Gardin took it. "What's this?"

Crag said, "I never counted it. But it's something over half a million dollars—or wastepaper. Here it's wastepaper, so you might as well have it. Now get going on that unloading, all of you."

Gardin seemed puzzled, almost reluctant, but the others worked faster, probably, than they'd ever worked at anything before, probably afraid Crag would change his mind.

An hour later, standing beside a tarpaulin covered pile of supplies that represented everything the ship could spare, he watched it go.

He felt dull inside, neither happy nor unhappy. This was the way it was going to be. This was his world and here he was going to stay until he died or was killed. He'd be lonesome, sure, but he was used to that. And this was infinitely better than the cesspools of corruption that Earth, Mars and Venus had become. This was a tough world but an honest one. It was, and would be, *his* world. During the time the alien who had created this world had been in Craig's mind, he'd learned enough to make the world for which Crag was fitted.

It was getting dusk as he watched the speck out of sight, too late to do any more brick making tonight. Almost time to start a fire; he might as well get it laid and ready to light. He started toward the pile of wood the women had gathered.

But he'd taken only a step when the voice of the alien spoke in his mind.

"You did right, Crag. Like yourself, they were rebels against a bad society. But rebellion had made them decadent rather than tough. I knew when I first contacted their minds that they wouldn't stay."

"I should have guessed myself,' Crag said. "Except Gardin—I thought he might make it."

"He came closest. He might have if he'd been alone, not weakened by having the wrong woman."

Crag laughed. "Is there any such thing as a *right* woman?"

"Your subconscious mind knows that there is, Crag. One and only one for you."

Anger flared in Crag. "You dared—"

"Don't forget, Crag, that happened when I'd just revived you from being dead, before I knew you resented invasion of privacy. I told you I'd never enter your mind again and I have not. I can put my voice, as it were, in your mind; but what my mind receives from yours is only what you speak aloud or what you deliberately project to me as a thought. So I know only what was in your mind then—but I doubt that it has changed."

Crag didn't answer, and the voice went on. "Do you remember what happened to Judeth, Crag? The disintegrator, yes. But before that happened I had studied her mind and her body; she was the first of the three of you on that asteroid that I studied. But I did study her and I have not forgotten the position of a single atom or molecule. And those atoms, even after disintegration of her body, were still there. It was easy to segregate and preserve them."

"For what?" Crag almost shouted. "She's dead!"

"So were you, Crag. What is death? You should know. But I saved her, for you. Until you were ready, until you came to me as I knew you would. It was a relatively easy thing to restore life to your body and a relatively difficult one to replace every atom in every molecule of—"

"*Can* you? Are you sure?"

"I already have. She's coming this way now; if you turn you'll see her."

Crag turned. And stood trembling, unable for the moment to think, let alone to move.

"You won't need to explain anything to her, Crag. I put knowledge in her mind of everything that has happened. And I can tell you that she is not only willing but able— But I withdraw from your mind now, from both your minds. I'll let you tell—"

But Judeth was in his arms by then and Crag had quit thinking or hearing thoughts in his mind.

ABOUT THE AUTHOR

FREDRIC BROWN was born in Cincinnati in 1906, and was educated in the public schools of that city, and at Hanover College. Among his numerous successful novels are: *The Screaming Mimi*, *The Far Cry* and *Night of the Jabberwock*. He is also well known for his short story collections, among them *Nightmares and Geezenstacks* and *Space on My Hands*. He died in 1972 in Tucson, Arizona, where his wife, Elizabeth, still lives.

OTHER WORLDS
OTHER REALITIES

In fact and fiction, these extraordinary books bring the fascinating world of the supernatural down to earth from ancient astronauts and black magic to witchcraft, voodoo and mysticism—these books look at other worlds and examine other realities.

THE EXCITING REALM OF STAR TREK

☐ 2151   **STAR TREK LIVES!** $1.95
        by Lichtenberg, Marshak & Winston
☐ 2719   **STAR TREK: THE NEW VOYAGES** $1.75
        by Culbreath & Marshak
☐ 11392   **STAR TREK: THE NEW VOYAGES 2** $1.95
        by Culbreath & Marshak
☐ 10159   **SPOCK, MESSIAH! A Star Trek Novel** $1.75
        by Cogswell & Spano
☐ 10978   **THE PRICE OF THE PHOENIX** $1.75
        by Marshak & Culbreath
☐ 11145   **PLANET OF JUDGMENT** $1.75
        by Joe Haldeman

THRILLING ADVENTURES IN INTERGALACTIC SPACE

BY JAMES BLISH

☐	12591	SPOCK MUST DIE!	$1.75
☐	12589	STAR TREK 1	$1.75
☐	10811	STAR TREK 2	$1.50
☐	12312	STAR TREK 3	$1.75
☐	12311	STAR TREK 4	$1.75
☐	12325	STAR TREK 5	$1.75
☐	11697	STAR TREK 6	$1.50
☐	10815	STAR TREK 7	$1.50
☐	12731	STAR TREK 8	$1.75
☐	12111	STAR TREK 9	$1.75
☐	11992	STAR TREK 10	$1.75
☐	11417	STAR TREK 11	$1.50
☐	11382	STAR TREK 12	$1.75

Buy them at your local bookstore or use this handy coupon for ordering:

NEW!
STAR TREK
FOTONOVELS

Each fotonovel authentically recreates an episode from the TV series—with hundreds of full color action photos and actual dialogue, plus a glossary, cast listing and notes.

☐ 12564	City On The Edge Of Forever	$2.25
☐ 12726	Where No Man Has Gone Before	$2.25
☐ 12689	The Trouble With Tribbles	$2.25
☐ 12744	A Taste of Armageddon	$2.25
☐ 11349	Metamorphosis	$1.95
☐ 11350	All Our Yesterdays	$1.95
☐ 12041	The Galileo 7	$2.25
☐ 12022	A Piece of the Action	$2.25
☐ 12021	The Devil In The Dark	$2.25
☐ 12017	Day of the Dove	$2.25

Buy them at your local bookstore or use this handy coupon for ordering:

OUT OF THIS WORLD!

That's the only way to describe Bantam's great series of science fiction classics. These space-age thrillers are filled with terror, fancy and adventure and written by America's most renowned writers of science fiction. Welcome to outer space and have a good trip!

☐ 11392	**STAR TREK: THE NEW VOYAGES 2** by Culbreath & Marshak	$1.95
☐ 11945	**THE MARTIAN CHRONICLES** by Ray Bradbury	$1.95
☐ 02719	**STAR TREK: THE NEW VOYAGES** by Culbreath & Marshak	$1.75
☐ 11502	**ALAS, BABYLON** by Pat Frank	$1.95
☐ 12180	**A CANTICLE FOR LEIBOWITZ** by Walter Miller, Jr.	$1.95
☐ 12673	**HELLSTROM'S HIVE** by Frank Herbert	$1.95
☐ 12454	**DEMON SEED** by Dean R. Koontz	$1.95
☐ 12044	**DRAGONSONG** by Anne McCaffrey	$1.95
☐ 11599	**THE FARTHEST SHORE** by Ursula LeGuin	$1.95
☐ 11600	**THE TOMBS OF ATUAN** by Ursula LeGuin	$1.95
☐ 11609	**A WIZARD OF EARTHSEA** by Ursula LeGuin	$1.95
☐ 12005	**20,000 LEAGUES UNDER THE SEA** by Jules Verne	$1.50
☐ 11417	**STAR TREK XI** by James Blish	$1.50
☐ 12655	**FANTASTIC VOYAGE** by Isaac Asimov	$1.95
☐ 02517	**LOGAN'S RUN** by Nolan & Johnson	$1.75

Buy them at your local bookstore or use this handy coupon for ordering:

Bantam Books, Inc., Dept. SF, 414 East Golf Road, Des Plaines, Ill. 60016

Please send me the books I have checked above. I am enclosing $_____ (please add 75¢ to cover postage and handling). Send check or money order —no cash or C.O.D.'s please.

Mr/Mrs/Miss_____

Address_____

City_____State/Zip_____

SF—11/78

Please allow four weeks for delivery. This offer expires 5/79.

Bantam Book Catalog

Here's your up-to-the-minute listing of over 1,400 titles by your favorite authors.

This illustrated, large format catalog gives a description of each title. For your convenience, it is divided into categories in fiction and non-fiction—gothics, science fiction, westerns, mysteries, cookbooks, mysticism and occult, biographies, history, family living, health, psychology, art.

So don't delay—take advantage of this special opportunity to increase your reading pleasure.

Just send us your name and address and 50¢ (to help defray postage and handling costs).

BANTAM BOOKS, INC.
Dept. FC, 414 East Golf Road, Des Plaines, Ill. 60016

Mr./Mrs./Miss_____
(please print)

Address_____

City_____ State_____ Zip_____

Do you know someone who enjoys books? Just give us their names and addresses and we'll send them a catalog too!

Mr./Mrs./Miss_____

Address_____

City_____ State_____ Zip_____

Mr./Mrs./Miss_____

Address_____

City_____ State_____ Zip_____

FC—9/78